# Murder Below The Waterline

## The Mag and Clara Balefire Mysteries

BOOK THREE

## REGINA WELLING
## ERIN LYNN

# Murder Below the Waterline



ISBN- 978-1-953044-10-5

Cover design by: L. Vryhof

Interior design by: L. Vryhof


http://reginawelling.com

http://erinlynnwrites.com


First Edition

Printed in the U.S.A.

# Contents

# Acknowledgements

Thanks to all the usual suspects.

You know who you are!

And to Theresa Crouse who has the best lipstick! Thank you! We couldn't have done it without you!

# Chapter One

"I changed my mind. I don't think this is a good idea after all." Margaret Balefire cast a wary eye over the cobbled-together piece of floating death she'd helped her sister build for the town of Harmony's 'Anything Goes' flotilla race. "It doesn't look seaworthy."

Hagatha Crow, the third member of their crew, scoffed. "We're not going to sea, you weenie. We're just taking a lazy float down the river. You can swim, can't you?" The ancient witch cackled and completed a hop-and-roll motion onto the precarious craft, leaving her walker, complete with tennis-ball-covered feet, standing on the dock.

She'd probably enhanced the aerial feat with the subtlest wisp of magic, but Mag had to give it to her—it was still impressive. Even though Hagatha was more powerful than any three regular witches put together and about as predictable as a tornado, she was older than dirt; Mag refused to be outdone and boarded the craft.

Mag wished she could tell old Hagatha to take a flying leap off a short broomstick, but it had been her idea to fashion a boat out of an old brass bed and four

1

claw-footed bathtubs in the first place. She figured it would be a good play on their store, Balms and Bygones.

Instead, she climbed into the contraption, scowling when it rocked and wobbled as she settled in. What was the worst that could happen, anyway?

Nothing good ever came of asking that question, but she'd survived much worse in her years as a hunter of rogue magic; surely a flotilla race wasn't going to kill her.

"All set?" Clara Balefire winked at her sister, tugged at the bottom of her life vest to settle it more firmly into place, and handed Mag a paddle.

Mag glared at her sister as she took it. "If I die, I'm going to kill you."

Clara smirked, and with more grace than she normally showed, leapt from the dock to the foot of the bed. Springs creaked and Mag didn't bother hiding a smirk when the bounce-back effect nearly tossed Hagatha into the river.

"Nobody's going to die, but I might have you fitted for a crown if you're going to be such a drama queen." Clara tossed over her shoulder.

Shoving the awkward craft away from the dock took all of Clara's concentration and a bit of assistance from Mag.

"We're supposed to paddle across, float past the judges panel, then get ourselves into position at the starting line," Clara said, focusing on moving in the right direction.

Big Spurwink river, fed by a convergence of smaller tributaries, was wide and deep where it flowed behind the downtown section of Harmony.

Once past the narrows just south of town, the banks spread in a gentle curve to create a slow-moving basin making that section the ideal spot to hold a flotilla.

The requirements for inclusion were simple: If it floated and had at least a three-person crew, it qualified. The tendency to stray toward the ridiculous was one of the things that made Harmony special, and the event drew tourists and residents alike.

Hunkered down on her side of the bed, Mag dipped her paddle into the space between the two bathtubs on her side and waited for Clara to settle into a similar, opposite position. At the head of the bed, Hagatha manned the tiller.

"Easy now," Clara grinned at Mag, "and go." It took half a minute for the motion to smooth out, and then the boat settled and they were off.

"This first bit is the tricky part." Shoulders bunching, Clara paddled harder to help turn the craft upstream. "There's just enough of a current to make it a chore, but after that, it's a walk in the park. She's going to float better than that raft of trash Penelope and her minions entered."

For the past few years, Penelope Starr had been gunning for the position of High Priestess of the Moonstone Circle, a public organization instituted by Hagatha during the pre-suffrage era. Despite her best efforts, she'd only managed to take over the civic side of the organization.

The Circle's counterpart, the male-run Brotherhood of Badgers, was established by one Evaniah Johnson shortly after the Moonstones came to prominence because he couldn't stand the thought of a group of women having any true voice in town proceedings. Being a strong woman and an even stronger witch, Hagatha retaliated and cemented the dynamic between the two organizations.

The current leader, a man named Perry Weatherall, wasn't a complete jerk, but he hadn't done anything to reduce the friction, either. There was always a level of rivalry going on behind the scenes.

After hearing Hagatha's firsthand account of the inception story, including the part where she'd hexed old Evaniah's droopy doo-dahs off, Mag declared her solidarity to the cause.

This year, the Badgers went all-or-nothing with a canoe crafted from duct tape and paper, while the Moonstone Circle boasted two entries in the flotilla. Hagatha captained one with the Balefire sisters as crew. Penelope captained the other.

Mag raised a brow, her doubts fading when the other witches floated by on a disaster made from empty milk jugs and laundry soap containers tied together with cotton clothesline.

Penelope and her bikini-clad cronies perched on top of the recycled raft, each wearing a wide-brimmed hat to keep the sun from pinking her smirking face.

Mag felt the tingle of magic lifting the hairs on the back of her neck and pointed a finger at Hagatha, "Don't do it. We're going to win this thing, and we're doing it without casting hexes at the competition."

"What's the fun in that?" Hagatha hmphed, but let the power subside. She did conjure a Viking hat, slapping it on her head as they made the final course corrections to pass in front of the tent where the judges waited.

Typically, the flotilla served as the morning appetizer for the main event, the Backcountry Paddle, a three-mile canoe race through the faster-moving waters between Dover and Harmony, but this year, things were different.

Kevin Cardiff placed second in this race ten years ago. As executive producer for the Trek Network, a low-budget Travel Channel imitator, he'd convinced his bosses to provide national coverage for the event. They were featuring Harmony, the flotilla, and the Backcountry Paddle on a special two-hour episode of *Round-Trip Ticket*, the network's highest-rated show that covered unconventional events in out-of-the-way destinations.

Footage of the flotilla would provide color for the canoe race coverage. Past national winners, including Kevin, had been drafted to judge.

And so, when the bathtub-pontooned bed boat passed by the cameras that were recording the action, Hagatha, in all her wrinkled glory, rose to her feet between the pillows, placed a hand on the arched brass headboard, and gave America her best Napoleonic pose.

"Sit back down, you old coot," Mag spoke from between clenched teeth, turned her face away from the judges, and contemplated diving overboard. "You're rocking the boat and you're supposed to be steering, not mugging for the cameras."

It didn't help her mood when the loudspeakers mounted on either side of the tent boomed out the commentary delivered by the co-hosts, a man's man named Matt Chase and his perky, blond companion, Grace Abbott.

"Here comes number seven," he said, mugging for the camera worse than Hagatha had. "Let's hope no one rolls out on the wrong side of that bed."

The joke wasn't funny, but Grace laughed at her partner as if he'd said something witty. Clara had read that the co-hosting pair were romantically linked.

It was her turn to speak, and she gestured toward them Vanna White-style. "Lucky number seven is sponsored by the Moonstone Circle, and also by Balms and Bygones, Matt. And two of the lovely ladies manning her are the owners. Looks like they've taken the bed-and-bath concept to a new level, Matt." Grace beamed, her tanned, glowing face lighting up the stage as Matt flashed her a besotted glance.

"The final entry of the day is made out of—I'm not sure what I'm seeing, Matt."

"PVC tubing, styrofoam, and tractor seats is what it looks like to me," her manly sidekick replied, squinting toward the next contraption. "Manned by Harmony's own Mayor McCreery, along with Chief Cobb and Officer Nye of the local constabulary."

Grace let loose a laugh that teetered on the precipice between genuine and rehearsed, "A formidable team, certainly. You'd know a little something about that, wouldn't you Matt?"

The next few announcements blurred past as Clara and Mag paddled like crazy to get into their starting position. If Penelope got splashed by some errant water, it wasn't on purpose. Much.

"Now," Matt continued, "when the race starts, contestants will have to paddle hard to get momentum. Once they pass the buoy marker, it's all about the steering. There's just enough current to carry through to the finish." He explained.

"Right you are, Matt. If they hit the marker with enough gusto, anyway. This is going to be fun to watch. And, here we go!"

At the crack of the starter pistol, Mag and Clara applied paddle to water with zeal. But no magic—that would have been cheating.

Mag was only eight years older than Clara, which is nothing in witch time. Usually. Mag had been a warrior and nearly died when an encounter with a rogue magical beast had gone horribly wrong. In an instant, the Raythe had stolen Mag's youthful appearance and a fair share of her vitality as well.

As she knelt on the colorful quilt, wisps of age-whitened, fuzzy hair fluttered in the wet wind where long, dark tresses should have blown, and wrinkles lined a face that should have been like Clara's, easing toward the lower end of middle age.

But Mag was stronger than she looked, and determined not to let Penelope Starr win. Penelope had tried to push her fanatical views on hiding magic from Harmony's non-gifted mortals so insistently onto the coven that she spurred Hagatha into rebellion—and Mag understood why. For thousands of years, witches had managed to live among humans with only a few, albeit famous, slip-ups.

How Penelope had garnered such support behind their coven leader's back was a mystery Mag intended to solve. She smelled a story that had nothing to do with Hagatha and everything to do with something Penelope didn't want made public knowledge.

Coven politics aside, Penelope just rubbed Mag the wrong way, and she delighted in torturing her in any way possible, big or small.

"Go, go, go," Mag urged needlessly and paddled for all she was worth.

"Whoops folks, we've got a sinker." The male announcer's voice came over the water, and Clara only had time for a quick glance to see which boat was out of the race.

It looked like the space-saucer brigade had capsized. Tied together by the handles, and wrapped in aluminum foil, the four saucer-shaped winter sleds weren't deep enough to keep from taking on too much water. An air horn sounded to let everyone know the rescue team had been deployed, and Clara kept on paddling.

"Don't worry, folks, everyone's safe and sound," Grace told the audience a few moments later, just as the final entry passed the buoy marker.

Tossing her paddle into the middle of the bed, Clara scrambled up to sit next to Hagatha. "It's all down to handling the rudder. Need any help?" Discretion might be enough to keep her from spending the next week as a frog.

"Take over if you've a mind to, little Balefire." The gleam in Hagatha's eye boded ill. "I'd rather sit up front anyway." The wizened old crone eased her way toward the footboard, leaving Clara to wonder if she should have left well enough alone.

Watching for subtle changes in the current that might push them along faster, Mag ignored Hagatha and kept an eye on the competition. "Jig left when I tell you," she said.

With Perry Weatherall at the helm, the Badger's canoe had shot ahead at the beginning of the race but was now a soggy mess and dead in the water. Hagatha chortled and flipped Perry the bird as the bed boat slid on past.

"You mean to port." Unlike Mag who cared little for sailing, Clara lived for the feel of skimming over the water.

"Whatever," Mag snapped. "Just do it. Now!"

Clara gave a little yank on the tiller, which angled the rudder—a toilet seat in its former life—turning the boat into the current. A gentle pull would have been better than the yank; a few gallons of river water poured over the edge of the port side tub.

"Jig right to even it out," Hagatha barked, leaning over the brass footboard to reach for the tiller.

Clara sucked in a breath, visions of the old witch falling overboard dancing before her eyes. "No! I've got it," she said, her heartbeat slowing a little when the old crone sat back down.

"We're good," Mag said. "I prepared a little something for emergencies." She flopped on her belly, reached up under the edge of the bed, and pulled out a battered, long-handled saucepan and a roll of duct tape. She grabbed Clara's discarded paddle and fastened the pan to the blade.

"I'll bail. Hagatha, you navigate."

"Let me." Clara made to leave her post, but the look Mag flashed warned her off. She took both hands off the tiller to turn them up in a gesture of surrender. "Hurry up, though. We're losing momentum."

"Trouble ladies?" They'd been so busy looking to port, they didn't notice Penelope and crew three lengths back on their starboard side.

"Why? Looking for some?" Clara retorted, an uncharacteristic bit of malice creeping into her tone.

"Hard right. Now!" Mag shouted over Clara's loaded response, and Clara yanked the tiller. The bed heeled into Penelope's path and picked up speed without taking on more water.

"That was just plain mean," Mag commented, but Clara couldn't hold back a little smile. A glance over her shoulder revealed a fuming Penelope and her befuddled crew.

"What? There was a branch in the water. Getting Penelope's feathers ruffled was just a nice side benefit."

A glance showed only one other contender for the win. McCreery, Cobb, and Nye looked like they were part of a three-man bobsled team. Tractor seats mounted on blocks of foam lined up one behind the other. The plastic tubing cut through the water with ease.

A full length behind, Clara steered the bed deeper into the middle of the river where the water ran the fastest and closed the gap by half, but she could tell the extra push wouldn't be enough to take the trophy.

"This race is turning vicious," Grace commented over the loud speaker, "And it's not over yet."

"It sure isn't," Matt replied, keeping his eyes trained on the remaining crafts, "One of them is going to win it by a hair."

"Ease her around that little eddy," Mag said, "and then keep the rudder straight. It's our best shot." As the girls navigated, Hagatha did the unexpected. Rising, she planted her feet, rested her thighs against the tall footboard, and leaned forward, still wearing her Viking hat, posed as if she were the figurehead of a ship.

A beautiful mermaid, Hagatha was not. Although her face did look like something dredged up from the bottom of the ocean.

"Where was she hiding that cape?" Clara asked, risking a glance at Mag. Deep blue velvet flowed off Hagatha's frail body and she assumed she'd conjured that, too. But there wasn't time to worry about it.

"We're witnessing showmanship at its best, folks," Matt announced with a smile on his handsome face, pointing to the old, fearless woman. "Now let's see them bring it home."

When the makeshift rig dumped out of the last of the rushing water and made for the finish line, McCreery and his crew looked to be only a few feet in the lead. The plastic pontoon boat hugged the water, skimmed across the surface where the bed-and-bathtub boat settled in deeper but had the benefit of weight giving it momentum.

"Watch out!" From her elevated height, Hagatha saw it first, a jagged stone just peeking above the surface and right in the path of her competitors. Clara caught sight of it, but could only cringe as events unfolded.

The plastic boat hit the rock, flipped up, and dumped out its passengers right as the Balefires and Hagatha eased across the finish line.

Air horns went off simultaneously, one signaling the end of the race, another alerting the rescue crew.

"Hagatha, take over here so I can paddle, please." Clara dragged on the tiller to heel the boat around and point it toward the dock, then scrambled into position opposite her sister.

Momentum had carried them too far to get back to the capsized craft in time to help, so they paddled toward the dock while watching to make sure everyone else was okay.

"Quit worrying," Hagatha said, waving a dismissive hand in the Mayor's general direction.

"Crap always floats." Whether she was referring to McCreery or Cobb was anyone's guess.

# Chapter Two

"How does it feel to win?" Grace aimed her microphone at Clara before she'd barely had time to get solid footing on the dock. A busy young brunette woman relieved her of her paddle, and with quiet efficiency, directed a couple of able bodies to secure the sort-of boat.

Raising a brow at such an odd question, Clara stuttered out that it felt fine, but her attention was more focused on the stretcher bearing one of McCreery's team. Someone should have seen that rock sticking up so close to the finish line and put a marker on it so nobody got hurt.

Meanwhile, her lack of enthusiastic response had turned the camera's attention to her teammates, and Hagatha in particular.

Considering the old witch looked like a wizened monkey wearing a cape and a Viking helmet, who could blame them? Her face animated, Hagatha gave a blow-by-blow description of the race that sounded a lot more exciting in retrospect than it had been while it was happening.

"Nearly came a cropper, we did, just before that last push. Water's low, I reckon. It's been drier than normal this year. Funny weather." Something in her tone caught Clara's attention and she shared a look of foreboding with her sister.

Anything Hagatha deemed funny would be of the peculiar rather than ha-ha variety.

"If you'll follow me to the judge's tent, we'll award the prizes," Grace said, a little overwhelmed by the whole odd mix that was Hagatha.

Angling up at a curve, the path ran around the edges of the unimaginatively named Spurwink Park, which boasted little more than a few picnic tables and a gazebo before widening out into a parking lot big enough for a few dozen cars. The lot was cordoned off to make space for the television crew, the judging tent, and spectators, and even the heat billowing off the square of pavement couldn't put a damper on the festive mood.

Food trucks lined the grassy verge behind an open-sided canvas pavilion, and competing scents perfumed the air. Tourists and townsfolk mingled, lounged on blankets, or spent time trying to get on camera.

After all, this was a chance to be on national TV, and for some people, that seemed to be enough to make them lose their minds.

A trio of young witches Mag dubbed Double Bubble, Toil, and Trouble sashayed back and forth across the parking lot with one eye on the lens, and the other on the young, bearded fellow behind it. Like a well-oiled team, they managed to get in front of him at every turn.

Heads tilted, eyes wide and smiling, they pouted their lips, stuck out their hips, and tried every trick to draw the camera in their direction. Clara could have told them they were wasting their time, but what would have been the point?

Before she had a chance to nudge Mag and make a snarky comment, the young woman from the dock hurried over.

"My name is Jane, and I'm an intern with the production company. If you'd come with me, we have a release form for you to sign, and then we'll get you ready for the winner's ceremony. It's taking place at the Oarhouse Inn, and all the participants are invited to a banquet afterward."

"A release form? For what?" Mag ignored the rest of what Jane had said, the thought of signing something that implied a restriction of any sort immediately raising her hackles. Mag enjoyed freedom above all other rights and didn't relish the idea of relinquishing it in any way.

Jane raised an eyebrow, "You're going to get an inside look at production, and with that comes sensitive information. We can't have you leaking our evil secrets, now can we?" She said with a wink. "It's standard, and the same will be asked of every attendee."

"Fine, fine." Mag acquiesced, following Jane toward a tent reserved for administrative matters. She spent a solid five minutes scrutinizing the document before finally signing her name with a flourish. Clara, on the other hand, scribbled her autograph without a second thought.

"Psst." Mag's elbow tagged Clara on the ribs as they exited and made their retreat. The inn Jane had mentioned was positioned a bit further downstream from the park, just a short walk along the riverside trail.

"You're going to give me a permanent dent if you keep doing that." Rubbing the sore spot, Clara considered retaliation.

"Quit being a baby," Mag said. "Don't be obvious about it, but look at the roof of the tent."

To the untrained eye, it looked like dozens of overly large hummingbirds perched along the ridgepole. That alone would have been remarkable enough, but these weren't hummingbirds at all.

They were a charm of honey pixies Hagatha had secretly imported from the Faelands. And there were far more of them than the Balefires remembered seeing the last time they'd visited Hagatha's oasis-like compound in the woods.

Mag lowered her brows. "Where is she?" She scanned the area, but there was no sign of the pixie whisperer. She turned back toward the tent just in time to see the entire charm lift off, dive toward the water, then wink out of existence, a sure sign Hagatha had done the same.

Maybe not the diving part, but the winking from one place to another, and from a public setting, too. Clara groaned.

"Long gone, I'd say, and I think it's time we paid the pixies a visit. Something tells me—"

"Don't say it," Mag pleaded as if not hearing the words would make them untrue.

"Hagatha's up to something." Finishing the sentence she had come to dread, Clara pushed a hank of waving chestnut hair behind one ear with a weary hand. "And why that surprises me every time, I'll never know."

If Mag and Clara had realized the extent of the power struggle going on between Hagatha and rest of the witches in the town of Harmony, they might have given the place a wide berth.

Penelope strove to nix the use of magic completely in the town, but as high priestess, it was Hagatha's job to lead her coven in the ways of their heritage, not to suppress them.

And so, the two factions had squared off and turned the town of Harmony into their private battlefield, with Mag and Clara drafted as unwitting referees. Combined with the drama between the Moonstones and the Badgers, rural life had become far more exciting than either sister had expected.

Clara's eyes narrowed. "What are the chances she's been letting them breed unchecked?"

Following a mating ritual so perilous few males survived, honey pixies reproduced like bunnies. Eager, active bunnies.

They'd been hunted nearly to extinction in their native lands, and Hagatha had taken it upon herself to save the species. Or so she said. Both Balefire sisters suspected her of murkier, must less philanthropic motives but had yet to prove it.

"We can just pretend we didn't see that and go home, right?" Mag asked, hoping against hope. "If we're stuck going to some banquet later, I'll need a breather." An introvert at heart, she preferred solitude to crowds and had already had her fill of socializing for the day.

"Tempting." With the excitement of the race and the anticipation of the banquet later, even a social butterfly like Clara felt the strain. "But you know we're going to go look. For curiosity's sake alone. And we can't bail on the winner's ceremony tonight, much as I know you'd like to."

Blessing the ability to travel from one place to another in the wink of an eye, the sisters stepped behind a tent where they wouldn't be seen, then focused their intent on finding the pixies and magically skimmed through space. Touching down lightly, they realized they were in a secluded clearing far enough away from town to make accidental visitors unlikely. Hagatha had chosen her spot well.

"Ouch!" Clara took a step forward, then a hasty one back, rubbing her nose. "She's put up a barrier, and it's powerful."

"Doesn't bode well." Grim-faced, Mag explored the magical boundary. "You think she's trying to keep people out or the pixies in?"

"If it's the latter, it isn't working very well. There must have been a hundred of them on that tent." Frowning, Clara considered the repercussions if the camera crew managed to get footage of the charm taking off or landing.

"Hagatha!" Mag yelled. "Let us in." The *or else* was implied.

A moment dragged by and Mag pulled out her wand and tested the barrier for the best counter-spell. She shook her head at Clara, then called out a second time. If Hagatha didn't want them in, it would take more than just a few seconds and a quick spell to break the barrier.

"I'm old, give me a minute." The sound of shuffling feet and Hagatha's creaking gate of a voice came from the empty space right in front of the sisters.

Part of the barrier fell like melted wax flowing over glass to reveal Pixieland in all its glory. Hagatha had been busy, and it showed.

"For the love of Danu." Mouth hanging open, Mag couldn't take it all in at once. A solid half-acre of rainforest nestled amid the sturdy Eastern pines and looked like the kind of place where an Oompa Loompa might go on vacation.

Taller than a man who made his living lobbing balls through hoops, a pile of pink granite chunks rose through the center of the secluded grove. In the spaces where the stones met, miniature planting beds birthed a riot of delicate blossoms and fragrant grasses.

Jewel-toned petals in ruby and amethyst sparkled under a perpetual layer of dew, their scents heady and powerfully sweet.

The last time Mag and Clara had visited the pixie's oasis, a witch-made fountain cascaded over the peak and ran in rivulets down to the lagoon ringing its base.

Since then, Hagatha had leveled up and expanded the ecosystem. Four additional mountains ranged through the clearing. Fluffy clouds ringed each apex and rain fell in a steady shower over each set of southern and western slopes.

Rainbows arced the spaces between their hives and the shimmering pools where pixies lounged and tended their young. So many young. Their bodies no bigger than the end of a pinky finger, their tiny faces flushed and pink and dewy.

Dripping honey, the basketball-sized hives swung on spiderweb ropes looped over low-hanging branches, each one a glittering jewel of insect wings and woven flower petals. Each one collecting delicate drops of rainbow nectar.

Heavy moisture rose from the soil like a miasma, plastering Clara's clothes to her body, and making it difficult to even breath. There was no shortage of rain there, and it didn't take a genius to figure out what Hagatha had done.

"You've been playing with the weather and diverting the all the rain here, haven't you?"

Like a child caught with her hand in the cookie Jar, Hagatha tried to deflect. "They need a wet climate to make the most potent honey. It's for the babies."

"And that's another thing. You know you can't let them keep breeding like this." In the hot and humid conditions, Mag's hair went from dandelion fluff to something similar to a copper pot-scrubbing pad that had gone through a wood chipper.

Hearing the declaration, an angry buzz went up from the pixies and a dozen or so took flight to land on Hagatha and glare at the newcomers. If there was one thing Mag had learned during her days hunting magical predators, it was that small things often posed a larger danger.

Oh, and don't mess with mother anythings.

In this case, they were dealing with a hefty dose of both.

The last thing she wanted was to face down a pack of pissed off pixies when she had no idea what sort of magic they were capable of throwing around. Draped in feathery bodies Hagatha looked determined to lead the brigade.

"Look." Diplomatic as always, Clara smiled winningly. "Stop co-opting the rain. There are farmers whose crops are just as important to them as your pixies are to you. Surely you can understand how they feel."

Besides, weather magic carried a heavy karmic balance, so Hagatha must be feeling the strain by now. At her advanced age—and it was said she counted her years in the thousands, but no one could know for certain—such powerful magic must be exhausting.

"If they're going to stay," she continued, "the pixies will have to adjust to a drier climate." There would be no talking Hagatha into sending her charges back to their homeland—that much was obvious by the set lines of her lips and the fire in her eyes.

Clara hoped she could broker some kind of deal that would bring much-needed rain to Harmony without making an enemy of the one witch in a hundred-mile radius that could wipe the floor with a Balefire. Magically speaking, of course.

Physically, Hagatha would be hard pressed to outrun a turtle on a downhill slant.

While the old witch thought things over, the forest held its breath, and so did Mag and Clara.

"I guess you're right." Raising a gnarled hand skyward, Hagatha made a complicated, oddly graceful gesture, and the atmosphere immediately lightened, much of the moisture released.

Another angry buzz sliced the air.

"Settle down, you lot!" Hagatha stifled the sound with her own angry outburst. "Between you and me, they're getting to be a bit of a handful," she confided.

"Send them back where they belong," Mag said, still a little amazed at the sheer numbers. "You're not doing them any favors, you know. If acculturation increases the adaptive mechanism too much, you risk creating a subculture that can't exist when they're reintroduced to their native habitat."

When Clara stared at her a little slack-jawed after her impassioned speech, she scowled. "What? I know stuff. You think I don't, but I do."

In recent weeks, Clara had come to realize her sister kept mum about more than just the Raythe-hunting parts of her past. Who would have expected the gruff Margaret Balefire to be harboring concern for things like carbon footprints and the anthropological ramifications of bringing honey pixies between worlds?

"When have I ever said you didn't?" Clara rolled her eyes. "Now it would be great if you could repeat that in layman's terms."

Mag sighed and dumbed it down, "Introducing the pixies to a different culture might make it impossible for them to return home, and worse, given the speed at which they reproduce and that they lack a natural predator—let's just say we're going to be overrun with pixies in no time flat."

Shaking off the pixies clinging to her hair and clothes, Hagatha gestured for the sisters to follow and stomped back the way the Balefires had come. Once outside the curtain, she reversed the opening, and when it had sealed, spoke in a low tone.

"I've been adding a little extra something to their feed. There won't be any more babies, but they don't need to know that. Easy to fool, they are, when you keep them fat and happy. Be a long time before they notice unless some idjit comes along and lets the cat out of the bag."

To be discussing birth control options for Faelands creatures seemed to Clara bizarre beyond the telling of it, but Mag had questions.

"What are you using? And how did you figure out the formula?"

Mag's interest calmed Hagatha's natural tendency to become defensive, and Clara wisely kept silent while the pair discussed herbal infusions and the merits of fresh over dried passionflower extractions for calming.

The sun was drifting toward the west when she finally announced it was time to get ready for the banquet.

"You know, Hagatha's not so bad when you get to know her," Mag noted with a smile. It seemed the longer they stayed in Harmony, and maintained contact with Hagatha, the more respect Mag had for the elder witch. Clara dreaded the upheaval that combination might make, exponentially increasing the problems she already had to deal with.

"Not so bad, huh? Remember that next time we get called to ride herd on one of her shenanigans." Linking her arm through Mag's, Clara smoothly shifted them home.

# Chapter Three

Harmony, while quaint and downright picturesque, traded on providing tourists a vacation experience with a timeless feel. Big Spurwink River had drawn in early settlers with the promise of unlimited fresh drinking water, and later facilitated the manufacture and transportation of lumber.

But now, in the throes of the technological revolution, with mainly the tourism trade keeping the town afloat, local businesses were forced to up the ante if they wanted Harmony to compete with larger coastal destinations.

To that end, the owner of the town's old inn, The Harpy's Hideaway, decided to change its name to the more appealing—or, some would say, boring—Oarhouse Inn & Tavern.

To some of the older Harmony residents—Hagatha included—the formal change didn't matter. They'd call it Harpy's for another hundred years, at least.

Gone were the thick, creeping vines that had once covered two-thirds of the inn's facade. Instead, whitewashed siding contrasted with a cobbled stone turret that veritably screamed 'rustic charm'. A brand new, in-ground pool, strategically hidden from the building by a strand of conical juniper trees, provided just enough luxury to garner an extra star on the inn's rating.

"I don't see why we have to go to this banquet in the first place," Mag grumbled as she and Clara pulled into the overflowing parking lot across the street from the front entrance.

Clara rolled her eyes for about the fiftieth time since she'd helped Mag pick out an outfit that didn't look like it came from the rag bag of a 1973 housewife.

In the end, Mag would end up having a good time and forget she'd ever objected to attending in the first place.

"Because it's fun. Remember fun? And we're going to get to be on television. You'll finally have something to put on the DVR besides cop shows and medical dramas. If I have to watch one more fake doctor perform a contrived-for-tv operation, I'm going to cancel the cable."

"Keep threatening me," Mag retorted, "and I'll charm the television to play med school footage on a loop for a fortnight."

Clara kept ticking off the points on the upside. "You know the co-hosts, Matt and Grace? They're a couple in real life. Very hot and heavy."

"What?" she demanded, brows raised when Mag shot her a dirty look for pulling their magic-powered VW minibus into the handicapped space. "It's the only space left and you do carry a cane. Now, where was I? Apparently this Kevin Cardiff is the executive producer and director for "Round Trip Ticket" and wants to turn the coverage into a two-hour retrospective of the Backcountry Paddle Race."

Clara figured if Mag knew some of the players, her penchants for picking up good gossip and people watching might make the evening bearable.

"It's been ten years since they had it in Harmony, and Kevin competed," Clara explained. "He was the second place winner the last time if memory serves."

"Second place just means first loser." Mag retorted.

"You are the most jaded person I've ever met. Good Goddess, Maggie. It'll be good for tourism revenue, which means it will be good for *our* business. Hop on board, before I push you over the side."

Mag rolled her eyes, "Go right ahead and try."

Clara ignored her and forged on. "It's an interesting story because two of the judges actually were the winners of that race. Jason Trumbell—he's the quiet one with the wavy hair and blue eyes—and Grant Garnett, who runs the design division of Rockopotamus Canoes Kevin and Matt were favored to win, but Jason and Grant took the race in a last-minute upset. They came away with an endorsement deal as part of their winnings."

"Scintillating. How do you know all this anyway? Have you been stalking the hotel or something?" All Mag had wanted was to beat Penelope in the flotilla. If she'd known it would lead to all this fraternizing and hobnobbing, she'd have kept the bed-and-bath boat idea to herself.

"I looked it up on the Internet. I figured having a few nuggets of information might help if any of the cast or crew showed up at the shop. It was all in the name of research."

Mag wasn't buying it. "It was all in the name of gossip."

"Besides," Clara wheedled, "There's an open bar, and you've been begging me to try the lobster rolls here for weeks."

"Stop drilling; you've already struck oil," Mag said, pushing the door open. "As if I had a choice, anyway, considering who's on the guest list. Penelope and her minions will be talking about this for months, if not longer, and I'll never hear the end of it if I refuse to attend."

Mag hated the fact that Penelope felt her position as leader of the Moonstones' civic side also meant she held dominion over the coven itself, even though the honor of high priestess was still Hagatha's to hold, and would be until the day the ancient witch died. Considering how many witches had come and gone during Hagatha's reign, neither Balefire was willing to take bets on how many more years she had left.

Once inside the inn's front entrance, all of Mag's reservations melted away as she inhaled the scents of lemon, beeswax, and tung oil that only an expert antiques-dealing witch could have delineated from beneath the heavy cloud of competing aromas wafting from the kitchen.

"Look at these side tables, Clarie, they're absolutely mint. And probably cost one, too." Mag ran her fingers lovingly over the mahogany finish on a set of Victorian butler's tables.

Clara's untrained eye couldn't see what all the fuss was about. "They're nice, but I wouldn't know the difference between that one and a knockoff from Pottery Barn."

"And this is why you make bath products and I stock the antiques." Mag grinned, finally in her element. "I'm going to see if I can find someone who can give me the name of their dealer. We could use a few more high-end pieces for the shop, and I'd love to get my hands on—"

"First place winners!" a lanky lad sporting a patchy attempt at a goatee barked in the sisters' general direction. He'd poked his head out of a swinging door and motioned for them to follow him. The did, and found themselves positioned behind a stage that faced the banquet room adjacent to the front lobby.

"Janie," he ordered, "get Tonya and tell her to bring her kit. These two need a spruce in the hair and makeup department before the camera rolls." He spoke into a headset that seemed like overkill, considering Jane was standing less than three yards to his left.

"Whoa there, Skipper. Pump the brakes. No need to accost the locals, especially two lovely ladies such as these," boomed a voice from behind Mag and Clara.

"Kevin Cardiff. Executive producer and director." A hand the size of a baseball mitt closed over Clara's and pumped it twice before doing the same with Mag. The man moved with all the eager enthusiasm of dog in the awkward stage where the brain still says puppy, but the body is fully grown.

"Nice to meet you." Few men carried enough height to make Clara feel dainty, but she enjoyed the rare occurrence. "I'm Clara and this is my—this is Margaret." She still hadn't gotten used to referring to Mag as her mother, but the visual difference in age left no other option. Fortunately, Mag enjoyed using the farce to her advantage enough to keep it from becoming a point of contention.

The man named Skipper, which Clara vehemently hoped was a nickname and not the poor boy's given moniker, valiantly attempted to hide a scowl, and would have succeeded if Kevin hadn't added a second jab for good measure. "You're not an executive producer yet. Still have a lot to learn. Like bedside manner, for one. Am I right, ladies?"

"Skip!" Jane's voice had an echo since she was standing right there, and it also came clearly through the microphone. "Holly wants you out back, ASAP."

Skip blanched, his eyes darting back and forth between the intern and Kevin as if unsure whose needs were more important. At Kevin's exasperated nod, he scurried through the door where Jane had just disappeared.

"It was nice to meet you, ladies. If you'd like to visit hair and makeup for a little pampering, it's just down that hallway, second door on your left. I believe the third member of your crew is already in the chair."

Rather than go through the process of having their faces painted by a stranger, Mag and Clara ducked behind a screen and applied something halfway between a glamour and a magical makeover.

"I thought we looked good enough when we got here." Mag fluffed her fuzzy white hair. "Now let's go see what they've made of Hagatha."

They found the old witch engaged in a staring contest with a determined-looking woman who held an orange tube in her hand.

"It's just a little mascara." The makeup artist wisely kept her distance. "I wasn't going to poke you in the eye, and kicking me in the shins wasn't very nice."

Exchanging a glance, Mag and Clara hastened to flank Hagatha before things got out of hand.

"I think they're ready for us. Thank you for—" When Clara got a look at Hagatha's face, she couldn't finish the sentence. She'd seen corpses look more lifelike than the old witch did now. "Anyway. Thank you."

It was all she Clara could do to hold back a snort of laughter, and she risked a bout of public magic to clear away the worst offenses. Foundation at least a shade darker than Hagatha's skin had settled into every wrinkle and made the slash of blush on her cheeks stand out like pink stripes.

"Do I look pretty?" Hagatha asked.

"Come on, they're calling our names." Adroitly avoiding the question, Mag's eyes danced with humor.

"And now, we're pleased to present the first-place winners of Harmony's annual Anything Goes flotilla race!" Matt waved his arms with a flourish while his co-host, Grace, sashayed across the dance floor of the Oarhouse's banquet hall and ushered Mag, Clara, and Hagatha into the center of the space.

Grace batted her eyelashes in Matt's direction, then returned to his side, her feet positioned perfectly in front of the masking-tape marker stuck to the floor. Matt's hand rested on the small of her back in an intimate gesture.

Kevin observed the scene, his face contorting into a scowl as he yelled, "Cut!" to halt the action.

"Grace," Kevin instructed, "We're changing positions. You stick to stage right, and Matt, you take stage left."

After several more incarnations of the introduction, Kevin seemed satisfied, though his jovial mood had all but dissipated.

"Are they about done leading us around like prized show ponies?" Mag muttered in Clara's direction. "We won, it's done, and now I'd like to try one of those lobster rolls everyone keeps talking about."

"Hush!" Clara elbowed Mag in the ribs and pointed toward the front of the stage where Hagatha now held court. "The on-screen portion of the evening is nearly over, and then you can eat your weight in shellfish for all I care. You're missing the best part."

Having nearly shoved Grace off the platform, Hagatha cupped her gnarled fingers into a wave and saluted the crowd as if she'd just been crowned Miss America.

"Has she been drinking?" Mag whispered out of the corner of her mouth, causing Clara to snort.

"Everyone, please join us in celebrating the kickoff of this year's Backwater Paddle. Eat, drink, mingle, and have a lovely evening." Grace flashed a toothy smile at the gathered group, tossed another back in the direction of her co-host, and situated herself off-camera, leaving Hagatha to continue preening.

Matt made eye contact with Clara and Mag from his position at the other end of the stage, and he looked ruefully between them and Hagatha as if begging for help. Clara made a move to comply but stopped when Mag grabbed her arm.

"Hold on, this is too fun. I want to see what happens next."

Finally, after a few awkward moments, the three flotilla judges escorted Hagatha to her table while exchanging grins they assumed went unnoticed by the seemingly-senile old woman.

"Your friend is a tad eccentric, no?" Matt sidled up behind Mag and Clara and chuckled into their ears.

Clara watched Grace's gaze flick past Matt and light on something or someone to the rear of the stage. A frown wrinkled her brow, and her eyes narrowed slightly. When the cameras stopped rolling, she headed in that direction without a backward glance.

"That's an understatement. They'll have to edit that end part if this winds up on *Round-Trip Ticket*," Mag muttered.

"A lot you know. This is exactly the kind of thing that ends up in the promo teasers," Clara said, nodding her head sagely.

Clara chatted with Matt for another minute before Mag pulled her away toward the table where Hagatha waited.

"Stay here, we'll fix you a plate, Hagatha," Mag promised, her eyes roving the room in search of the celebrated lobster rolls.

Typically reserved for events like wedding receptions and anniversary parties, the banquet hall was painted a neutral shade of cream and a half-dozen antique crystal chandeliers shed soft light over the room. Tables draped in indigo linen surrounded a central dance floor, and a matching buffet table lined a wall of windows. A covered patio offered shade if anybody wanted fresh air, and a grassy expanse led to a boat launch where a lone canoe swayed in the gentle summer breeze.

Mag marched on past a display of photos depicting the last decade of canoe-race winners, loosing a sigh as her sister paused their mission to get a closer look.

"I'm starved, Clarie, what's the holdup?" She demanded.

Clara rolled her eyes, "Relax, you're not going to waste away." She pointed to a photo in the center, then back toward the judges' table conveniently located near theirs. "That's Jason Trumbell, ten years younger."

It was a perfect shot capturing a shining moment of victory, but not one that had anything to do with a canoe race. There he was, on bended knee in the winner's circle, his face flushed with something more than the excitement of winning.

A young woman beamed down at him with tears glittering in her eyes, one hand in his, and the other clutched to her heart.

"Isn't it romantic?" Clara sighed. "He won twice that day."

"Yeah, it's sweet. Now can we please get in line before the lobster rolls are all gone?" Mag turned back toward the buffet.

"Over here, we have the second-place winners," Clara explained, pointing to more pictures.

"What's your point, Clarie?"

Clara huffed out a breath and shoved her sister toward the seafood with a bit more force than necessary. "Nothing, Maggie. Remind me never to take you to a museum. When did you become so impatient? Oh, wait, how silly of me. You've *always* been this way. You'd think after a couple centuries I'd already know that."

"You'd think." Mag snagged a fat shrimp and popped it into her mouth. It must have passed the test because she loaded a few more onto her plate.

"Now I see where Jinx gets it." Clara shook her head, thinking of Mag's feline familiar, who would give one of his nine lives for a morsel of shellfish.

Mag shot her a look of derision and resisted the urge to start a food fight right there in the Oarhouse dining room. But only because she didn't want to waste such good food.

# Chapter Four

Plates filled to overflowing, Mag and Clara passed one to Hagatha, settled into their seats, and proceeded to eavesdrop on the judges' table without a shred of remorse. In a town the size of Harmony, everyone already knew most of their neighbor's secrets, so an influx of fresh fodder was always welcome and usually considered long overdue.

"So, old buddy," Grant Garnett said to his old partner, Jason, "what have you been up to for the past few years? Last time we saw one another, you had a beard so thick I hardly recognized you. Glad to see you've cleaned yourself up." He shoved a mixed drink that was far more whiskey than soda into Jason's hand and clapped him on the back, smiling.

Jason took a swig, made a valiant effort not to screw his face up into a grimace, and set the cup back down onto the linen-draped tabletop. "I bought a place up near Bangor a few years back. Took an outside sales position with Hancock Uniforms that keeps me busy. How's the family?"

"Good, good. We're expecting our third in a few months, and Lesley has insisted on keeping this one's gender a surprise. She claims since we've already got a boy and a girl, we're prepared for either. Which I thought meant we wouldn't have as many supplies to buy, but the nursery looks like a storage closet, and I've seen enough yellow and green baby clothes to make me wonder if she's bought out an entire department store. But, I suppose things could be worse."

"Good for you, man. I'm happy for you and Lesley. You're both very lucky." Jason replied.

"Kevin naming Rockopotamus Canoes as the sponsor for the piece on the Backwater Paddle couldn't have come at a better time. It's my last hurrah before life turns into round three of diapers and spit-up."

A shadow of envy crossed Jason's face. "Lesley's okay with you being gone for a whole week?"

Grant nodded, "She's not thrilled with how much I travel, but she's a team player. And besides, there's talk about canceling the race if the water level keeps dropping. After that cop blew out his knee today when they hit that rock, they're worried about liability issues."

"They must have had everyone sign insurance waivers in order to participate." The claw from a two-pound lobster split and sent a chunk of shell across the table as Jason squeezed the cracking tool with too much force.

"I'd assume so," Grant agreed, "But being televised and all, there'd be negative feedback if anyone got hurt. Besides, if they do cancel, I'll get to go home sooner than expected."

As if on cue, a petite woman with blond hair cropped close to her head stalked past the judges' table, "Don't you dare jinx us, Grant Garnett! The show—and the race—must go on. Didn't your mother ever teach you if you don't have something nice to say, don't say anything at all? Forecast calls for rain, and rain it shall. Now, have either of you seen Kevin or that little brunette intern? I asked her to go get—oh, never mind, neither of you is any help whatsoever. Janie!" She yelled into the wireless microphone dangling from her ear and rushed off toward one of the unmarked doors leading to the kitchen.

"Who's that, Miss Know-It-All?" Mag prodded her sister, who merely shrugged and continued to munch on a delectable piece of shrimp.

Penelope, seated across from Mag and a bit closer than necessary to Perry Weatherall, piped up. "That's Holly Hightower. She's the PR rep for *Round-Trip Ticket*. You know, public relations."

"I'm aware of what PR stands for, thank you Penelope," Mag grumbled, earning an eyebrow raise from Perry, which could have been construed as either reproachful or amused depending on the effect Penelope's advances were having on him. She couldn't quite tell, yet, but was having a hell of a lot of fun observing the brazen seduction attempt.

Now that the pressure of being on camera had lifted, the guests from Harmony were able to relax and enjoy themselves. But it didn't escape Mag's or Clara's attention that the cast and crew still seemed tense.

Skip cast furtive looks in Kevin's direction whenever the figure-eights he was pacing into the floor orbited him close to the judges' table, and Holly's mouth never stopped moving for more than five seconds. She spoke alternatively into a cellular phone and her headset, occasionally barking orders at Jane, whose ugly black-rimmed glasses kept slipping down her slender nose. Each time she pushed them back into position, her gaze darted toward the judges' table and then quickly away.

"That Holly needs a drink." Mag commented, "Or maybe a sedative. She's vibrating at a very high frequency."

"You would be too if you had to do her job," Matt said and winked at Mag as he sailed past their table and joined Grant at the next one over.

Hagatha leaned over and quipped in a tone low enough for only the Balefire sisters to hear, "Seems to me like she needs a good piece of—"

"I beg of you," Clara interrupted, "Don't finish that sentence."

Shrugging, Hagatha turned her attention back to where Penelope had further diverted Perry Weatherall with a strong margarita and the release of an extra button on her already low-cut top.

"Why hasn't that niece of Hagatha's come to pick her up yet?" Mag muttered under her breath to Clara. "Her lips are getting looser with every sidecar."

Clara shook her head, "Romilda Crow is probably off somewhere counting her lucky stars someone else is dealing with old Haggie tonight. It's actually kind of sad if you think about it."

But Mag wasn't thinking about it and had no intention of wasting any sympathy on the girl. Hagatha would do as she pleased whether Romilda attempted to intervene or not, and seemed quite happy running amok.

Just then, Grace lived up to her name, gliding off the stage as if she were floating. She tapped twice on the microphone, sending a boom through the speakers that perked everyone's ears.

"If I can have your attention, please. Thank you all for coming tonight and for your participation in the flotilla today. We appreciate your willingness to take part in the Backwater Paddle, and how welcoming you've all been to the *Round-Trip Ticket* team.

"I've been told the last shuttle bus has arrived. It will make a stop at Spurwink Park, then one at the center of town, and end its trip back at the Riverside Motel. Of course, the bar here at the Oarhouse will remain open for a few more hours, and you're all welcome to stay as long as you like."

She paused for dramatic effect. "Personally, I need my beauty sleep, so I'll be calling it a night." Grace smiled self-deprecatingly at the titters of insistence that she needed no such thing, but her eyes glittered with something deeper. "Good night everybody. Thank you again."

A flurry of activity began, and Mag started to rise from her seat.

"Sit down, we're not going anywhere yet," Clara said, pulling on her sleeve. "With the shuttle bus out there, we'll wind up sitting and waiting for who knows how long. Have another shrimp cocktail and keep your panties on."

Mag plopped back down in her chair and scooped a shrimp off Clara's plate.

Kevin appeared through the kitchen door with his eyebrows pressed together in an expression that made the fine lines in his forehead stand out. When Matt caught his eye and gave a nod, he made his way over to the table with a detour past the bar and pulled out a chair.

"You work too hard," Matt told him, waving his hand in a dismissive gesture. "Let the crew handle things for a bit, and enjoy yourself for once. Grant here has just been regaling us with tales of his exploits as an ambassador for Rockopotamus Canoes. He and Jason had quite the adventure, from the sounds of it."

Kevin made an effort to let the tension fall away, but his smile seemed a little forced at first. "It's too bad we missed out on that, but I'd say we've done okay for ourselves." He gestured at the festivities going on around them.

Grant exchanged a grin with Jason. "Too bad, indeed. If Lady Luck had been on your side, you'd have snagged those poly-core paddles instead of us. Then maybe you'd have been the pair to tromp through beach country with half a dozen boat models at your feet. Youth and stupidity," he said, shaking his head. "What a combination."

Jason joined the group with a plate from the buffet just as Kevin downed a third shot of whatever he was drinking. "Wasn't in the cards, man," he said with a hint of a slur, "Told the rep to give them to you so it would look like they helped you win the race."

"Better switch to coffee, Kev." In the silence following Kevin's cryptic comment, Matt's hearty advice sounded overly loud.

"That was awkward," Mag pronounced after a heavy moment. "And now I think I need another one of those lavender mojitos. Fancy a trip to the bar?" She hauled Clara out of her seat without waiting for an answer.

The pair made their way through the crowd, which had thinned considerably by then, only to find the line at the bar trailing all the way back to the nearly empty buffet spread.

"Follow me," Clara instructed, marching out an open set of double doors and into the night. She led Mag across the flagstone patio toward another, almost hidden and completely deserted drink cart.

Mag grinned, "How did you know this was here?"

"Penelope's a total wino. I heard her telling Double Bubble about it." Clara muddled mint leaves in tall glasses along with a spritz of lavender syrup, then added rum, lime juice, and topped the whole thing off with seltzer. She garnished each with a slice of lime and handed one to Mag, who sipped with appreciation.

The sisters spent a moment quietly dissecting Penelope's shortcomings before turning to retrace their steps. Looking the other way, Clara nearly knocked Mag over when she stopped short. Two people engaged in a private conversation beneath the low-hanging branches of a weeping willow beside the patio had caught her attention.

Almost hidden in the shadows, Kevin and Grace appeared to be in the throes of a whispered disagreement, her arms crossed in front of her and his gesticulating wildly.

Mag inched her way closer, curiosity grinding out all sense of propriety, in an attempt to catch a snippet of their conversation.

"You're being nosy," Clara warned, but followed on her sister's heels anyway.

Mag snorted, "And you're the pot calling the kettle black."

"It wasn't a criticism. Sheesh."

Before they could get close enough to hear anything of interest, Grace stomped off in the direction of the inn. Kevin heaved a sigh, pulled a pack of cigarettes out of his pocket, and sat down on the grassy embankment. He stared out toward the little boat landing and watched the water lap against the riverbank as smoke drifted from his lips.

Leaves rustled, and they turned. A figure approached from the trail that arced down to the entrance of the inn's pool. Deep shadows fell in mottled shapes between the areas touched by spotlights mounted on the back of the inn. Holly the PR rep stepped out of the darkness, and the light from one of the beams highlighted her grim expression. She rounded the corner and stopped for a moment as if deciding which path to take, then turned toward the river and disappeared.

The sisters looked at each other and shrugged, then retreated back to their table to collect Hagatha. Perry was beginning to look more uncomfortable than intrigued by Penelope's advancements.

"Penelope, why don't you let poor Perry breathe?" The statement reeked of Mag's disdain, and from the look on the younger witch's face, had the desired effect of shaking her confidence.

Clara didn't exactly feel sorry for Penelope, but she chided Mag gently anyway, "That was kind of a cheap shot."

"For the love of tiny pickles, Clarie. She can take it. She sure dishes it out."

"You're probably right, but I think that's your parting jab. I'm ready for bed. Let's go." Clara rose and began to collect her things. "Hagatha, do you want a ride?"

The old woman shrugged, "Sure, but wouldn't it just be easier for me to—" She blurted, earning a cross look from Penelope and a poke in the ribs from Mag.

Clara pushed her toward the exit, "You're not going to skim out of a public place for the second time today. Why don't you just hop a broom and make a production out of it? And that was a joke, before you get any ideas."

"You're leaving already?" a voice boomed from behind Clara. When she turned around, Matt Chase was bent casually over the back of a nearby chair, the impish grin on his handsome face making clear the reason he'd been offered an on-screen position with the Trek Network. "The party's just getting started."

Shaking her head, Clara politely explained it was time for them to be getting along.

"At least let me walk you to your car." A piece of cake held tightly in one hand, Mag graciously accepted Matt's proffered arm and allowed him to lead her toward the exit. Clara smiled internally, wondering whether Mag was sweet on the man, despite her usual insistence that she could manage well enough on her own, thank you very much. Hagatha linked her hand through Matt's other arm, and the odd trio walked to the parking lot with Clara in the lead.

"You ladies really showed some ingenuity. That float was inspired. Reminded me of Bedknobs and Broomsticks. I half expected one of you to turn that brass knob and disappear to a faraway land." Matt had no idea how easily the three witches piloting the craft could have done just that. "Where's your car? Or did you fly here on a magic carpet or something?"

Clara pointed toward the old VW bus that could have qualified as Matt's "or something" since the engine only operated thanks to a complicated locomotion spell. "Thanks," she said. "I can take it from here."

"Very well. You three have a wonderful night. We'll be down by the river tomorrow, taping interviews for the show. Come on down if you're interested. We always love to hear what the locals have to say." Matt winked as Clara settled herself into the driver's seat.

"Thanks for the invitation. you enjoy the rest of your evening." Clara waved as she backed the VW into the road and headed back toward home.

# Chapter Five

"Clarie, I can't find my cane." Mag burst into Clara's bedroom above their shop, Balms and Bygones, and roused her sister from a dead sleep. Pyewacket, Clara's familiar, flattened her ears and glared at Mag before hopping daintily off the bed and trotting out the door. Halfway down the stairs, the pitter-patter of cat paws turned to a stomp as Pye transitioned into her human form.

"Sounds like a personal problem to me." Clara snapped, pulling the pillow over her head. Morning was not her favorite time of day, and it wasn't like her sister had come bearing the cup of steaming coffee that might have softened her usual grouchiness. "You probably left it at the Oarhouse last night. We'll take a ride back there on our way to the set. But I'm not going anywhere without breakfast."

Mag snapped her fingers and shot Clara an impatient nose wiggle. "There, the table is set. Waffles, coffee, bacon, and fruit. Now if you don't hurry it up, you'll have to eat it out of a Ziplock bag while I drive."

Clara sighed, shooed Mag out of her bedroom, and magicked herself into an ankle-length white skirt with slimming vertical aqua stripes and a matching sleeveless aqua top. Hagatha's pixies had made this summer one of the hottest on record, raising hemlines throughout town, much to the delight of Harmony's male population.

She might only appear to be in her mid-forties—and the kind that might be called the new thirty at that—but two hundred and fifty plus years on earth had lent a certain amount of prudence to Clara's personality, and she wasn't about to flaunt herself all over town no matter how high the temperature rose.

Choking down a plate of waffles with strawberry jam and maple syrup faster than she'd have liked, Clara popped a strip of bacon into her mouth and poured her coffee into an insulated travel mug with a handful of ice while Mag tapped her foot against the hardwood floor impatiently. Jinx nabbed the rest of the bacon while adeptly ignoring Clara's steely glare and trotted off into the backyard.

"You could have made me a Pop Tart if you weren't willing to wait, you know." Clara admonished her sister as they headed out to the carport and climbed into the VW bus with Mag at the wheel.

Mag rocketed out of the driveway at a speed no normal VW bus could have managed, took a right-hand turn at the foot of the hill, and gunned it all the way until they pulled up in front of the Oarhouse, a cloud of dust in her wake.

"Subtle. Real subtle." Clara admonished, her knuckles white from holding so tightly to the armrest.

Mag duly ignored her sister's sarcasm and hopped out of the bus with a thump. The pair made their way inside and found the front desk abandoned, not a guest in sight.

Two of the inn's housekeeping staff, dressed in pale blue uniforms with starched white collars, huddled near a cleaning cart. One seemed to be comforting the other.

Something was wrong.

Like a bloodhound catching a scent, Mag toddled through a screened back door and followed her witchy senses toward the back of the inn, where raised voices signaled a disturbance.

A crowd had gathered around the edge of the inn's brand-new pool, the cluster of bodies obliterating Mag and Clara's view of whatever had caused the commotion. With most of the crew being housed at a cheap motel out on the edge of town, the only remaining Oarhouse guests were the on-screen personalities and VIP staff.

Mag shoved her way through them and knew she and her sister were about to become part of something sinister even before the police sirens wailed in the distance.

Face down in the crystalline water of the pool, a man's lifeless body drifted in the backwash of the filter like a forgotten beach ball.

"Whoa, there." Matt Chase stepped in front of Mag in a chivalrous gesture. "You might not want to see this."

Mag looked like a child next to the man, barely coming up to his waist, but he stepped aside when she leaned around him to get a better look. "Who is it?" She demanded.

"Don't worry, neither of us possesses what you'd call a delicate constitution," Clara assured Matt.

Matt's veneer of calm broke for a half-second, but he tried to compose himself. "It's Kevin," he choked out. "Kevin Cardiff, our executive producer and director, and my best friend."

On the other side of the pool, Grace huddled on the ground while a wide-eyed Holly tried to provide comfort. Somewhere in the gray space between shock and hysteria, Grace trembled, her slight frame quaking with each tear-soaked breath.

When Deputy Nye and Mayor McCreery emerged from the front of the inn, she let out a wail and buried her face in Holly's shoulder.

"We … Grace and I found the body," Holly explained to Deputy Nye, who looked like a fish out of water trying to pretend she was still swimming. "She's in shock."

Deputy Nye nodded, "Take her inside. I'll send one of the responders in to assess her condition. We can get her statement once she's calmed down. Can you handle that?"

Holly cast a panicked eye around the group of gawkers while Mayor McCreery acted in the absent Chief Cobb's stead, and ushered people away from the crime scene. "Can't someone else handle her? I'm going to have my hands full keeping a lid on the press. We're far enough from the nearest city that I've got a head start before the vultures descend. Matthew, can you please?" Holly implored.

"Of course." He slid a sad glance back toward the pool but led a still weeping Grace past Jane, the intern who seemed out of place as a guest given her status within the crew. She caught Matt's eye and reached out to give his arm a gentle rub on his way by.

"Stick around," Nye instructed as Holly pulled out her phone and stepped away from the crowd. "I'll need a statement from you as well. Nobody is allowed to leave." Holly waggled fingers over her shoulder to indicate she'd heard the order as she started a terse conversation with whoever had picked up on the other end of the line.

Mag and Clara watched, fascinated, taking in as many details as possible, and hung back waiting for the dismissal that never came.

Instead, Mayor McCreery approached the sisters with his eyes, as always, trained on Clara.

"Hello again, Clara. Margaret. Why is it that you two always seem to be on the spot when someone turns up dead? Do you have a police scanner, or a crystal ball or something?" He quipped.

Clara resisted the urge to return Mag's elbow to the ribs and instead turned wide eyes on the mayor. "Just a string of bad luck, I guess."

"At least we weren't the ones who found the body this time," Mag noted in an acerbic tone.

The mayor's mouth set in a thin line.

"True. Now, given your previous victories in the crime-solving arena, and knowing there's little hope you'll leave this up to the police, I'm going to say something that I don't want repeated. Ever. Understand?"

At twin nods, he continued, "Chief Cobb is on medical leave, and our only other experienced detective can't get back from his family vacation for at least a week. Trek might be a small television network, but it's a television network all the same, and they're going to expect this case to be solved quickly and quietly."

McCreery double-checked that his officer was out of hearing range.

"Deputy Nye, proficient as she may be, is out of her league. Any fool could see that. And so, you have my blessing—as long as you keep yourselves safe—to do whatever magic it is you ladies do, in the interest of figuring out who killed this man. With any luck, someone will confess or have left enough physical evidence for a speedy arrest. But if not, I'd like to know I have an ace in the hole. Or two, as the case may be."

"Of course, Mayor Mc—I mean Mr. May—I mean Norm. Anything we can do to help." Clara finished lamely.

The mayor smiled, and Clara wondered if she'd just given him false hope of the romantic variety, having finally assented to using his first name after several requests to do so.

"Clara and Norm, sittin' in a tree. K-I-S-S—" Mag taunted once he was out of earshot.

Clara cut her off and shot her a dirty look. "Let it go. There's a dead man thirty feet to our right. Don't you think the situation deserves at least some level of respect?"

"Of course I do, Clarie," Mag snapped, "But he can't hear us, and my ability to set aside my emotion for a moment doesn't change the fact that I have every intention of figuring out who killed him. And on a side note, doesn't it concern you that Mayor McCreepy makes a witchy reference every time he talks to us?"

"You know he doesn't have anything concrete," Clara softened toward her sister, but kept her tone brusque, "I'll know if he does, and I'll take care of it. For now, it looks like we're on another case."

"Sure does. If this one goes well, we ought to start charging the police department for our services." Mag watched Lynn Nye doing her level best as the emergency team lifted Cardiff's dripping body out of the water. The poolside evidence had long since been contaminated by onlookers, leaving only the body to be examined for untainted clues.

Bolstered by McCreery's tacit approval, the Balefires picked their way around the edges of the group, then slid—or in Mag's case, shoved—their way through to the position closest to the action.

The county coroner squatted on one side of the body while Lynn knelt on the other. Nye's hands trembled a little, Clara noted, as she pulled on a pair of sterile gloves.

"I won't know until I get him on the table, but my best guess is he's been in the water since last night and I'd put the window for the time of death somewhere between 1:00 and 3:00 am."

"And the cause of death?"

Gently lifting the collar of Kevin's shirt away from his neck, the coroner pointed to an ugly mark, red shading to purple.

"Ligature marks indicate he was strangled before falling or being thrown into the pool."

"So we're most likely looking for a man. A woman wouldn't have the strength for something like this," Lynn hesitated before touching a gloved finger to the dead man's throat where the livid bruise stood out against the pale, almost blue skin.

"Oh, a woman could do it under the right circumstances." Mag stepped forward and drew Nye's attention to a deck chair lying on its side close to the edge of the pool. "There was an open bar last night, and I know for a fact Kevin had been drinking. We saw him knock back a few during dinner."

To illustrate her point, Mag grasped the coroner's arm and guided him toward one of the chairs ringing an umbrella-topped table.

"Let's say he was sitting here, thinking deep thoughts." Looking around, Mag spotted one of the guests who had exactly what she needed, and without apology, she grabbed the woman's purse—a shoulder bag with a long strap.

"All it would take," she said, tossing the purse handle over his head, "is the element of surprise." She planted her knee high up on the back of the chair before yanking on the purse hard enough to snug the strap against his neck. "And a bit of leverage."

Sober, in daylight, and with a warning, the coroner's struggles weren't as effective as expected. Mag hung on while his face went from smug to terrified, and then she let go.

"She's right, it could be done." He rubbed his neck and popped to his feet, knocking the chair over in his haste, and gave Mag a look that landed somewhere between respectful and wary.

# Chapter Six

Inside, all of the guests had gathered in the east wing parlor, where Mayor McCreery facilitated the search of each patron's room while an officer took statements.

"Assuming everyone is present and accounted for," Mag whispered to Clara, "we've got a fishbowl full of suspects. Kevin was killed after the final shuttle left for the motel with the rest of the crew, which means everyone in this room was here during the murder."

Besides a couple of out-of-towners who appeared more frustrated at having been detained than concerned about the loss of a man's life, only the cast, judges, and primary crew loitered in the parlor.

Matt sat on a tufted armchair, his head in his hands, while Jane sat across from him, her back ramrod straight. Every few seconds she cast a worried look in his direction. Several times, she opened her mouth to speak, then closed it again without saying a word.

Clara nodded in agreement, "As morbid as the thought is, strangling is usually a crime of passion or self-defense. I'm guessing the former since there didn't seem to be any evidence of a fight. Your little demonstration made me think, though. If the murderer used stealth to get in a similar position, that speaks to premeditation."

Mag lifted a shoulder. "Everyone here had the opportunity, and when we find out what was used to strangle him, we'll have a better idea who had the means. For now, we just have to consider everyone a suspect."

The pair found a quiet corner and, after a short conversation, chose their tasks.

"You'd think if McCreery wanted us on the job, he wouldn't have left us out of the interviews." Digging around in her bottomless purse, Clara finally handed Mag a pair of wireless earphones.

"Get as close as you can to the office door, and when you're in place, give each earpiece a quick tap. You should be able to hear everything being said while they're conducting the interviews. I'll see what I can glean from idle chatter," Clara instructed.

Holly and Skip, Clara's first targets, stood in a quiet corner and carried on a hushed conversation about how to proceed with the shoot.

"How do they expect us to go on when our producer/director was brutally murdered? We're on a countdown to when this hits the national media and I'll do everything I can to get ahead of it, but it's going to be a nightmare." Cold-blooded business, with just the barest hint of remorse—that was Holly.

"I wonder who they'll send as a replacement. Probably not me, even though I know the job and I'm already here." Now, Skip, he sounded excited about the remote possibility, and maybe a little apprehensive, Clara thought.

Probably came from working with people who demanded the shoot continue at all costs. The fact its executive producer could no longer be counted among the living was just a detail. Clara shook her head at the insensitivity and took some small comfort in the fact that she had no part in that business.

Moving slowly toward the office door, Mag tried to keep a low profile. As she passed by them, Jason and Grant separated themselves from the rest of the Trek staff. The two settled into seats on the other side of the room and waited to be called into the office.

Grave-faced, Grant twisted his wedding ring and shot his former opponent a sympathetic look, which Matt returned while Jason simply stared into space.

Silence descended on the room except for when a periodic buzzing from Holly's purse prompted a mini-freak-out.

Clara suspected the woman would need a manicure once all was said and done if the frequency and intensity with which she was biting at her nails was any indication.

It felt like hours passed, but it was only minutes before Lynn opened the door and called her first victim in for questioning. Holly's eyes followed Matt's back as he entered the office to take his turn in the hot seat.

Mag shot Clara a wink from her post near the door and tapped the headphones twice to increase the volume, feeling little to no remorse about eavesdropping on an official police interview.

"Where were you between one o'clock and three o'clock this morning?" The deputy asked the question without mincing words.

Matt answered quickly, as though he'd prepared his response and was simply reading the lines out loud. "In my room."

"Were you alone?"

A moment of silence hung heavy in the air before Matt responded. "Yes."

"Can anyone verify your statement?" Deputy Nye prodded.

"No, unfortunately." Matt's voice sounded strained when he answered.

Nye declined to comment, and continued, "What was the nature of your relationship with Mr. Cardiff?"

"Technically, he's my boss. Was my boss, I mean. Unofficially, I've known him for over fourteen years. College roommates, racing partners, and friends. And no, we didn't have any issues that would have caused me to want him dead. In fact, in terms of my career, that's the last thing I'd want."

Mag listened while Nye asked the same questions again in a different order, and received similar answers in response. She found great amusement in the fact that Clara ended up with the more boring of the two assignments.

Clara was thinking along similar lines and wondered if she should make something happen to stir things up.

Across the room, Holly answered her cell phone in a muted tone, uttered a couple of uh-huh's and ended the call with a clipped, 'okay'.

"Skip," She motioned for him to return to her side, "You didn't hear this from me, but it looks like you're going to have to pick up where Kevin left off. My sources say the network isn't planning to send a replacement, so you're the acting executive producer and director."

Whatever Holly thought about that idea, she kept her face carefully blank. Skip, on the other hand, let a satisfied grin flare, if only for a moment.

"Corporate made it clear we've got to keep this as quiet as possible, finish the spot, and then return to the studio as soon as we wrap production. I—" She began, then with a pained look cut herself short, and began again. "Have them take your statement once Matty's finished, then head to the pavilion. Do not, under any circumstances, tell anyone anything about what's happened here. I will handle breaking the news once they've released me."

Skip nodded and stepped forward as an ashen-faced Matt emerged from the office. "Mind if I go next?" Without waiting for an answer, he strode across the room, clapped Matt on the back in lieu of a hug, and closed the door behind him.

Matt tried unsuccessfully to sidestep Holly, who waved him over to her corner of the parlor and began recounting her conversation with the bigwigs at Trek.

"The show must go on, that's what they said." She intoned, arranging her face into a neutral expression belied only by the fierce glow of her wide eyes. "And all that entails."

Matt's gaze fastened onto something across the room, but when Clara looked in that direction, all she saw was Jane, watching with interest.

"Holly," Matt said, mental exhaustion slumping his shoulders and dulling his expression. "I realize you're doing your job, but do you think I could have a minute here? This changes everything and I need to think about what to do going forward, especially about Grace. I think it's time to—"

"No!" Holly exclaimed. "If anything, it's the time to show a united front. Nothing changes, especially now. Grace is too distraught to think straight. She had to be sedated, and I won't have you upsetting her with this nonsense. Or setting me up for a public-relations nightmare. We can't afford even a hint of scandal."

"But..."

A loud buzzing noise outside the window behind Clara's seat obliterated what came next, and when she looked through the glass, it was into the eyes of a tiny honey pixie with lavender hair and a curious expression. "Shoo," Clara whispered, and watched Maypole zoom off into the sky.

When she returned her attention to the intense conversation, all she caught was a snippet of the end of Holly's sentence, something to the effect of, "Now is not the time."

Frustrated, she glanced in Mag's direction to see if her sister had noticed the tiny, unwelcome guest, but

Mag was so focused on watching Skip leave and Jason enter the office it would have taken an entire swarm to pull her focus.

The elder Balefire listened as Deputy Nye began asking Jason the same routine questions she'd required of everyone else. "Grant Garnett and I left the party together right around the time Kevin said he was turning in. Grant convinced the bartender to spot him a bottle of Jack Daniels, and we retired to his room."

"What did you do once you got there?" Nye asked, her tone neutral.

"We're old friends and haven't seen each other in years. We reminisced for a bit, maybe forty-five minutes, and then I returned to my room. The key card wouldn't work, so I came down to the foyer to ask for a new one. The redheaded night-shift clerk can verify the time. While I was waiting for her to program the key, I looked out the window and saw Kevin headed down that path toward the weeping willow, I assumed to smoke."

"And was anybody with him?"

Grant paused for a moment. "Not *with* him, but someone followed him, and it must have been a member of the cast or crew, because whoever it was had on one of those shiny Trek jackets.

"No, I couldn't identify the person. I didn't see their face, and from my vantage point, it was unclear whether it was even a man or a woman. I went back to my room and fell asleep shortly after." Nye asked a few more innocuous questions and dismissed him.

Nearly an hour later, after all the pertinent players had been thoroughly questioned, Mag and Clara were the only two people left in the parlor. "Okay, let's compare notes." Mag settled in next to her sister, pulling out a notepad that Clara hadn't even seen her use. She wondered idly if it was magic and had done its own jotting.

"No one knows anything," Mag said, rubbing her chin, "except everyone was lying about something. Matt was alone in his room, but I'm not buying that for a second."

"Well, he and Holly are hiding something, but I'm not sure it's related to the murder." Leaning in close, Clara repeated the highlights of Holly and Matt's cryptic conversation. "I'm not sure what it was all about, but it had to do with Grace, who had to be sedated, by the way."

"Deputy Nye wasn't any too happy about that, I can tell you. She wanted more than Holly's account of finding the body. Not much to tell there, either. She and Grace saw the body and screamed the place down. One of the staff jumped in and checked for a pulse, then called the police. We showed up not too long after, so the rest you know."

Mag consulted her notes. "Holly went on and on about how the police need to pass any and all information through her before it gets released to any media outlets. Blocked every question with one of her own and had Nye so turned around she didn't know her own name by the end of it."

She slid the notebook back into her pocket. "Skip knew nothing, saw nothing. Alone in his room, no one to corroborate. Blah, blah, blah. Same goes for Grant, though he did admit to having polished off half a bottle of whiskey. Jason saw someone in a Trek jacket follow Kevin after he left the party and headed toward the dock, and that's the most useful piece of information so far. Your turn."

"Oh, and there's one more thing," Mag added before Clara had a chance to launch into her own recitation. "Lynn's voice went all fluttery when she talked to Jason. I think she has a little crush on him. *Now, it's your turn.*"

Clara huffed. "You picked up a lot more than I did. In all that time, I learned the network put Skip in charge and handed down the edict that the show must go on. That's all I have." Clara threw up her hands in frustration. "You want to hang around or get back to the shop before Pyewacket and Jinx have a meltdown?"

Now that Mag had her teeth into another juicy mystery, Clara knew she'd have preferred to hang around and look for clues. What was the point, though, with Lynn and her crew beating the bushes for the murder weapon and every possible suspect having taken to their rooms?

"Come on, Maggie. Let's go home. Mrs. Green has been leaving open cans of tuna on her porch for Pye and Jinx, and every time there's a lull in business they start fighting over who gets the solid white albacore."

Clara worried that Pyewacket still held a grudge over the fact that after spending twenty-five years on her own, confined to cat form, she now had to pose as a common shop girl rather than work the magics with abandon. It didn't help that Jinx wasn't what you'd call stimulating company.

Mag nodded, "I have a shipment coming in this afternoon and we've got a lot of information to sort through. We might as well let the two of them run wild while we do it."

Their plan to go straight home was sidetracked when they spied a pair of figures pacing around near their bus in the parking lot.

Matt and Skip were carrying on an animated conversation. Even from a distance, the sisters could see Skip's demeanor had undergone a subtle change. Gone was the posture that reminded Clara of a petulant teenager.

"Looks like someone's got a swing in his step." Mag murmured.

"Yeah, and we both know what put it there." Clara sniffed, "Newfound power. Wait till he learns about the responsibility that comes along with it."

"Put a lid on it, Skipper." Matt spat, repeating the nickname Kevin had used, which did nothing to calm the guy. "I don't care what title corporate thrust upon you, and if you want the god's honest truth, I'd walk away right now if I wasn't under contract. It's a lousy tribute to the man when they continue on like nothing happened."

Skip, to his credit, made an attempt to diffuse the situation. "Nobody's expecting us to work as usual today. It'll be an official announcement. We'll pause for a day or so, and regroup."

"Yes, because a day or so is sufficient time to mourn." Matt's voice dripped sarcasm.

Skip took a deep breath, then released it. "It's still a business, Matthew. And I know Kevin was your friend, but the rest of us found him a little more difficult to work with. Rumor is, he's been on the way out for a while now. Holly said—" Upon noticing Mag and Clara's approach, Skip snapped his jaw shut, effectively cutting off the diatribe.

"I need you on set as planned," Skip said in parting. "And try to be strong, for the crew's sake." With that, he nodded once at the Balefires, got into a rented sports car Mag doubted he'd have the guts to actually use the way the Chevrolet goddess intended and sped out of the parking lot.

Matt attempted a smile and accepted Clara's hug with more emotion than she'd expected. "We're terribly sorry about your friend," she stated simply and sincerely.

"Thanks," Matt replied gruffly. "Don't pay any attention to Skipper there. Everyone else enjoyed Kevin's boisterous personality. Skip was just born with no sense of humor whatsoever, particularly when he's the butt of the joke."

"They really named him the executive producer?" Mag asked, disbelief coloring her tone. "Seems like there must have been *someone* more qualified amongst the staff." Her candor had less to do with her level of comfort with Matt, and more to do with who she was as a person.

She was unpredictable and swung from one extreme to another. One minute, she held onto her opinion tighter than an old biddy trying to lock down a fart in church, and the next, she let fly whatever she thought and damn the consequences.

Today, her thoughts passed right though her skimpy filter in a rush of verbal incontinence. Matt let slip the tiniest of smiles as Clara elbowed her sister in the ribs, "You'd think, but Skip's dad is one of the bigwigs, and this is the perfect chance for a justified display of nepotism. It doesn't matter anyway, at least not to me. All the joy I've taken from this job died with Kev."

His voice caught in his throat, and even though Clara knew getting emotionally involved with a potential suspect was the worst idea in the existence of murder investigations, she could feel her heart softening for the man.

"Pardon my frankness, but do you have any idea who would have wanted to kill him?" Mag asked. It wasn't often she asked anyone to pardon her for anything, and Clara suspected she wasn't the only sister who'd developed a soft spot for Matthew Chase.

Matt shook his head, and his fists and jaw clenched in unison, "That's what I don't understand. I know plenty of people who envied Kevin, but as I said before, he was a likable guy."

After a few more comforting platitudes, Mag and Clara piled into the Volkswagen and headed back toward town.

"Obviously Kevin wasn't as likable as Matt thinks," Mag postulated, "or he wouldn't have gotten himself killed. How can it feel like we've learned so much and yet still know so little?" She paused, mulling it over. "He made himself a target for someone. In my experience, mortal enemies don't usually come in singles. You tick off one person that much and chances are you've done it before."

Clara nodded, "It's pretty clear Skip didn't care for him, so he ought to go on the list. Though, that sounds like petty jealousy to me. He might have wanted Kevin's job, but if his dad's loaded, I doubt he needed the money bad enough to kill for the position. Add him to the possibles."

"They're all possibles, as far as I'm concerned, and Skip's pretty full of himself. Could have just been the prestige. Any one of them could have had a personal reason for getting Kevin out of the way. We've just got to figure out who had the most to gain." Mag ran down the rest of the people who were on site the previous night.

"Grace and Kevin sure didn't seem to get along. We saw that fight, and we also saw Holly skulking around." She narrowed her eyes. "Skulking women are always a red flag."

Clara rolled her eyes. "We skulked all day."

"My point exactly," Clara said. "We were up to no good, at least from their points of view. Now, back to business. Both Jason's and Grant's connection to Kevin seems tenuous, although Kevin just gave Grant a sponsorship on a national show. Killing him seems an odd way to say thank you."

"That's an understatement," Clara said, swerving to miss a pothole. "Besides, there's the person in a Trek jacket Jason saw following Kevin toward the pool. As far as staff goes, Jane is the only one left. Don't you find it odd that an intern gets to stay in the inn while the rest of the crew get shuttled off to Cheap Motel Land?"

She tapped her finger on the steering wheel. "Other than appearing a bit overworked, I can't see any reason to think she'd have wanted Kevin dead, though." Clara thought back to the way Kevin had interacted with the girl and decided there'd been no malice there.

Mag sighed, "Like I said, we need to know more. We'll go give an interview. We'll hang around, and do what we do best. Blend into the woodwork." Mag was beginning to get excited, and Clara could practically see the wheels turning as she turned over the details of the new challenge.

"You'd have to stop wearing paisley prints from forty-odd years ago if you want to blend into anything." Clara teased.

"Shut your piehole, Clarie, or I won't stop at Dairyland for your butter pecan."

Clara scoffed, "*My* butter pecan? You like it as much as I do. Just drive, Maggie." Clara hid the tiny smile that involuntarily curled her lip, happier—even under the macabre circumstances—than she had been in years.

# Chapter Seven

Every morning for the next three days, rain-soaked clouds sulked slate-gray over Harmony, weighting the air with promise but delivering none. By mid-afternoon, skies cleared to a searing, relentless blue that did nothing to lift moods.

With the water level of Big Spurwink dropping another inch, more rocks poked above her surface, putting the Backwater Paddle in jeopardy. Trek had finally worked out a shooting schedule, having believed the local weatherman who promised rain daily and apologized for its absence each night.

Mag and Clara were due to give a follow-up interview about the flotilla the next day, but without easy access to the crew, their investigation had come to a screeching halt save for Clara's social-media stalking.

At Balms and Bygones, Clara spent a busy morning selling sunblock and burn-relief cream while Mag replenished her diminishing stock of boating-related antiques. Whether it happened or not, the race hadn't hurt business.

She glanced around the storefront, crammed to the gills with antiques. Surprisingly, Mag had foregone the doilies she tended to put under everything; even she had to admit her Victorian sensibilities clashed with the nautical items that were flying out the doors.

"Good call on swapping out the inventory," Clara said. Pride at the compliment stained Mag's cheeks a pale pink. "You have a knack for retail."

Before Mag had a chance to puff up and brag, a series of thumps and crashes issued from the back room, which could only mean one thing.

"Hagatha." The sisters sighed in unison.

"Go, I've got the register," Pyewacket said, morphing from Siamese cat to golden-skinned human as she entered from the stairwell where she'd been sleeping in a patch of sunlight.

Ever since Hagatha had promised to replace Pye's tail with a ball of yarn, she'd determined to steer clear of the old witch whenever possible, and Clara expected to be subjected to a mini-rant once she and Pye were alone.

"You know, there are less destructive ways to pay someone a visit," Clara said, scowling as she and Mag set the space to rights with a few mumbled words and hand gestures. Hagatha's abrupt entrance had sent boxes of empty lotion tubes and Mag's box of unused doilies to the floor.

"I need your help," Hagatha said. Those four words must have burned like bitter bile on her tongue. "With the pixies." And three more to strike dread into the sister's hearts. Those blasted pixies.

"What have they done now?" Squinting, Mag demanded an explanation.

Like a felon running from the law, Hagatha glanced left and right, scanning the room for spies. With a whispered word, she cast a spell of containment around them.

"They've gone rogue. Kicked me out of the habitat just for starters." Her tone indicated worse news to come.

Chagrin looked out of place on Hagatha, and she rarely bothered to admit blame. If the honey pixies could drop a load of guilt on her, they must have done something awful. Mag and Clara prepared for the worst.

"Right smart little buggers, they are. It never occurred to me they were capable of extracting the essence of magic from a potion and using it for their own gain."

"Stop dancing around the truth and give it to us straight." That's the way Mag preferred to get bad news. All in a gulp so she could swish it around and taste the flavor before figuring out her next step. "How bad can it be?"

"Bad. They reinstated the weather spell." Hagatha paused to let that news sink in, and Mag rolled a hand to indicate she should continue.

"And they figured out a way to reverse the birth control potion." She grimaced, waiting for them to grasp the magnitude of the problem.

It didn't sound dire to Mag, though. "So they can get pregnant again. It could be worse, right? It must be close to the end of this mating cycle by now, and I know you don't have enough combustion powder left to go again. One, maybe two more days of being fertile and we're past the danger. Another handful of pixie babies at most, right?"

It was worse, and Clara had already figured out why. "No, Maggie. I think she's saying they reversed the spell."

"Didn't I just hear her say that? I might look old, but I'm not deaf." And then the implications hit, and Mag slumped down on a pile of boxes. "Are you saying they're perpetually fertile? That they no longer need a mating ritual?"

Mag's imagination supplied the mental image of a world gone feathery with millions of tiny bodies clogging the skies. Of worst-case scenarios, that was right up there.

"You've just set the stage for a Pixie Apocalypse—it will be the end of the world as we know it," Mag said, her voice going higher with each word.

Clara's face drained of color. "You have to send them back to the Faelands, Hagatha."

"Think I don't know that? I came here to beg you for help, didn't I? That ought to tell you something."

Desperation ate away at Hagatha's characteristic strength and turned her voice almost feeble. The uncertainty touched Clara's soft heart and cemented her resolve to make things right.

Mag held out a little longer.

"That's flattering." Sarcasm laced through the dry tone and arched eyebrow. "You made this mess alone, what makes you think we're going to pull your fat out of the fire again?"

If Mag meant to needle the older witch back to her normal, devil-may-care attitude, it worked. Hagatha's face changed, the twist of her lips turning feral.

"Oh, you'll help me. I know that well enough. You can't resist because you're Balefires and that's what you do. You ride in at the last minute to save the day and never count the cost."

Without mercy, the needle turned back on Mag, but it was Clara who prickled at the subtle insult.

"You say that like it's a bad thing, but someone has to stand for the innocent and I don't see you putting yourself in harm's way to help your fellow witch."

"So young, and so naive," Hagatha mocked. "You don't have enough age on you yet to take off those rose-colored glasses. You still think the world should be all sunshine and puppies."

"How can you say that like it's a bad thing?" Clara saw nothing wrong with sunshine, and puppies were cute. "I'm not going to argue with you over the merits of fighting against that which we would rather hide in the shadows. You are right, though. We'll help because what you've done affects the whole town."

Triumphant, Hagatha did a shuffling two-step before Clara pasted on a feral grin of her own. One that was slightly chilling to someone who had never seen the darker side of her before.

"But not for free. This time you're going to have to ante up."

When Mag would have jumped in with a comment, Clara stopped her with a barely perceptible shake of her head.

"Don't push me too hard, little Balefire," Hagatha warned.

"And don't forget you came to us for help." Pausing a moment to consider her options, Clara finally said, "I think we'll just put this one in the bank, and you can consider yourself in our debt. I wouldn't want to waste a favor from the great Hagatha Crow until we really need it, but when the time comes … you will not say no."

The end of the proclamation echoed out of Clara with the ring of truth and left Hagatha the choice of whether to agree and bind the pact or turn and walk away. Not being an idiot, she chose the former.

"Fine but—"

"No buts, no stipulations. Agree or we're done here, and you can fix your own mess for a change." Backing up her little sister, Mag's proverbial foot hit the floor. "The clock is ticking, and I assume pixies are procreating as we speak. Choose."

"Yes. I agree. Now, can we get started?" Hagatha ignored the way the air in the room shook when she took the deal.

Heady with having exerted her power, Clara still wasn't stupid enough to think Hagatha wouldn't push the boundaries, but for now, they needed a plan. For that, she turned to Mag.

"I can see the wheels are already turning, so what do you have in mind?"

If a tender heart was Clara's greatest strength, Mag's was an agile mind. Strategies formed in her head like building blocks, one piled on top of the other to form an unbreakable chain.

She gathered her thoughts and mused aloud. "The pixies like it here, and now that they feel like they're in charge, they're not going to want to leave. We need to find a powerful incentive to make them want to go."

An absent flick of Mag's hand sent a table full of packing supplies skittering elsewhere. Three chairs marched into place, and she directed Hagatha to one of them.

"We already know this isn't their ideal climate, so if we can override their hold on the weather, we can make them uncomfortable enough to want to leave. That's a tick in our favor."

Conjuring her version of a white board, Clara wrote in the air with a fingertip, and the word weather appeared. "What else you got?"

Well, there is one other thing," Hagatha said. "Before they booted me out"—the sour look on her face made it obvious it still rankled—"they'd been producing babies at an alarming rate, but nearly all of them are female. There aren't enough males to satisfy even a tenth of the females, and the ones that survived the mating ritual are starting to look a little worn around the edges. Some of the gals can get a little rough."

"And that was more than I ever wanted to know about pixie sex." Clara was two seconds away from clapping hands over her ears and singing the *la la I can't year you* song.

Honey pixies chose mates through a complicated and dangerous ritual that Hagatha had recreated in the center of a clearing ringed by towering pines. Mag carried some of the blame for it, though, since she'd been willing to trade grains of combustion powder for information that had helped solve a murder.

Hagatha had conjured from the earth a miniature volcano with slopes covered in beds of Faeland flowers. Amid the heady and conflicting scents of molten rock and fragrant petals, female pixies displayed their wares.

Powerful, dill-enhanced pheromones drove the males to foolish feats of virility that included a dip into the volcano's fiery mouth. Those who survived—and there weren't many—returned with singed wings to a harem of females and the frenzy of non-stop mating for the rest of the fertile cycle.

"Do you think messing with the natural order of things screwed up the birth rates?" Mag wondered.

With power came the responsibility to use that power wisely and for the good of others. It was the way of the blood witch. Not that Clara suspected Hagatha's cultivation of pixies had come from a place of ill intent, but the old witch had allowed her own desires into the mix. And now everyone would pay the price.

"Climb down off your high horse, would you? I thought I was helping the ungrateful critters if you must know. They've been hunted nearly to extinction in the Faelands, and I couldn't bear to see that happen."

"Noble, but you didn't answer the question," Mag pointed out.

"Don't need to, and I'm not eating crow for the likes of you. There's a lot we don't know about the ways of honey pixies, so the answer is maybe. Not that why it happened matters as much as what we can do for them. Or about them."

Grimly, and knowing her opinion wouldn't be appreciated, the anthropologist living in Mag's brain couldn't help pointing out, "If we send them home, and they no longer need the mating ritual designed to limit their population—" The sentence had so many possible endings, Mag couldn't choose one.

"But it's a chance we'll have to take. I can't see any way around it now. They need to go back, but how are we going to make that happen? I don't see forcing them as being a situation where we come out ahead. We'd need a powerful incentive to get them to leave willingly." Clara hit the nail on the head.

Hagatha thought for a minute. "I know a guy who could get me a dozen or so Indonesian water gremlins."

"No." Mag and Clara shut down the suggestion at the same time.

"Absolutely not." Mag insisted, "Where would it end? You'd bring in one predator to catch another and compound the problem. What we need is bait to draw them back to Faeland, and you've given me a good idea of what kind to use. Male pixies."

# Chapter Eight

Hagatha looked doubtful, "Didn't you hear me when I said they were hunted to near extinction? Where do you think you're going to find enough male pixies to service a charm this size?"

Apparently intent on hiding the true size of the charm, she spoke in general terms, which made Mag wonder how many pixie babies had been born since her last visit. "How long did you say the gestation period is for honey pixies?"

Doing nothing to alleviate Mag's suspicions, Hagatha skirted the question.

"Actually," Mag drummed wrinkled fingertips on the table. "It's probably just a rumor, but I've heard there is one place where a colony of males lives in seclusion."

"You're talking about the ascetic pixies of the Andruvian Mountains." Hagatha scoffed.

"Ascetic pixies?" Clara asked. "Like monks?"

"Yes, and while theirs isn't what you'd call a religion, it looks the same. They don't take vows of chastity, or poverty, but they are devoted to a very," Mag paused to choose the right word, *"particular* set of beliefs."

Clara's eyebrow shot up. "And what peculiar beliefs might those be?"

"Peculiar don't half describe it." Hagatha snorted and shared the kind of knowing look with Mag that made Clara want to bite through leather. She hated feeling left out.

"Peculiar, particular. In this case, it amounts to the same. They call themselves the Sacred Order of the Orbplant."

"You know what? I'm sorry I asked."

"It's a fascinating story, but the upshot is they consider themselves to be on an evolutionary track toward becoming plant-based life forms. And as such, beyond the bounds of the physical act of procreation. Which means—"

"Which means they're lousy bait for mating-obsessed females. Got any other ideas?" For someone who had come begging for help, Hagatha was eager to shoot down a possible solution.

"But they have the, um, how to put this delicately," Clara's face turned pink either with embarrassment or the effort not to dissolve into a fit of the giggles at having to ask. "Right equipment, right?"

Mag blushed and lifted a shoulder. "As far as I know, they do. If the group exists at all. There are more rumors than facts, but most of my sources are credible. You know, in and of themselves, anyway."

Clara remembered the Andruvian trumpet flower she carried as a keepsake in a potion bottle. Given to her, she'd intimated, by a male admirer at some time in the hazy past she had yet to share fully with her sister.

Could he have been the reason for Mag's interest in studying various cultures? Another question to add to Clara's growing list. At some point, she planned to loosen her sister's tongue with a few glasses of faerie-made Twinkleberry wine and get some answers.

Clara put the kibosh on Hagatha's suggestion of kidnapping the babies and transporting them back to the Faelands, even if it would work. No mother would do that to another and using the unsuspecting Andruvians as bait seemed the less diabolical of the two choices.

Hashing out a plan fell to Mag since strategy was her strength. Sifting through possibilities, she stood to pace the room.

The male pixies could just say no, and the mountain range was big enough for both groups to find a home. Or, there would be a population explosion that would draw predators from outlying regions and completely change the face of the Faelands ecosystem.

Or they'd fix it.

Slowly, a plan began to form. One that was two parts Pied Piper to one part mad scientist, with a little theater thrown in for flavor.

She began to lay it out for them in a series of terse sentences that were meant to put a damper on Hagatha but created the opposite response instead.

She grinned, grudging admiration shining in her eyes. "You're a hard woman, Margaret Balefire, and a crafty one. It *will* work and those pesky pixies won't know what hit them." The older-than-dirt witch attempted a booty shake that made Clara avert her eyes to avoid the risk of being scarred for life.

"Wipe that grin off your face." Mag narrowed her eyes and her voice dripped acid. "This was your doing, and it would serve you right if we left you to fix it on your own. The only reason we're helping is goddess knows what kind of mess you'd make in the process."

Turning to Clara, Mag said a single word, "Dill."

"Oh, I see." Clara clued right in. "We'll use dill to jack the female's pheromone levels up on high, connect to one of the mountain portals, and let the females draw the sect out of hiding."

It could work. It wouldn't be the nicest thing she'd ever done, but it could work.

"We'd need to concentrate the essence, enhance the dill to strengthen it enough, and blend several strains to get the best possible outcome." On her feet now, Clara stood in the doorway and sent tendrils of magic dancing into the back room where she stored her things.

Soil and compost funneled up, combined, and filled three pots to the brim. Water and a generous slug of something that sparkled and fizzed from a potion bottle followed. At the flick of a finger, a shower of seeds burrowed into the soil, and the pots flew to land on the hearth next to the Balefire.

Leaning down, Clara gently lifted a tongue of flame from the rest, formed it into a ball, and set it above the pots like a miniature sun.

"Give it an hour, and they'll be an inch high. Two days from now, I'll be ready to harvest. Now what?" The whole exercise had taken all of three minutes.

"On to the next problem," Mag announced and waited until all eyes were on her. "Breaking the pixie's hold on the weather before the canoe race has to be called off, and we never figure out who killed Mr. Muckety-Muck."

"I ran into Norm McCreery yesterday in Evelyn's, and he was so distracted he forgot to stare at my boobs for two minutes." Clara was dead serious but still cracked a smile when Mag hooted.

"Then you know he's gone over the edge of reason because they usually put a dumbfounded look of bliss on his face." Teasing Clara about the man she'd dubbed Mayor McCreepy lightened Mag's somber mood.

"Men love the ta-tas," Hagatha said, a look of nostalgia crossing her face. "Why I remember this one fellow—"

"No." Clara held a hand up to stop Hagatha from finishing any sentence that would put an image of the old woman's breasts in her head. Then she thought they probably looked like wrinkled peaches or prunes, and it was too late. The image was already there.

"Too much information," Clara said. "Just tell us the spell you used, and we'll go from there." It would take a few days before they could put the entire pixie plan into action, but the weather problem needed solving now. Preferably while letting the wretched creatures think they were getting away with their own scheme.

Hagatha squirmed at the thought of giving up one of her secrets. Witches of her age—not that there were many others, really—hoarded magic as if sharing a spell might cost them two.

Mag shrugged. "You don't want our help, that's your choice. I'll wash my hands of the whole thing and happy to do so." A threat Mag knew was empty the minute it left her lips. Hagatha knew, too, but couldn't see any way out of sharing.

"All I did was create a vortex. Kind of like a tornado, with the pixie habitat as the eye of the storm. It's pulling the moisture from the air and funneling it right to them." Hagatha explained.

"But that's so simple," Clara said, dumbfounded.

"The best magic always is." Hagatha nodded sagely.

Mag's eyes narrowed to slits, "Perhaps. Or maybe you made it so simple they were able to co-opt the vortex with ease."

"Fine. You're right. Is that what you needed to hear? They wanted more rain, so they added a boomerang effect, and now it's roaming all over town." Hagatha blurted. "It sucks up all the moisture, then returns to drop a load on the habitat."

"Make sure you get that on record, Clarie. Those words will never escape her lips again—of that I'm certain. Now, let's figure out what to do." Mag shot

Hagatha one more death glare and stalked out through the door.

Back inside the front room, Clara found Pyewacket still behind the cash register, steam practically shooting out of her nose. The ebony halo of hair that usually fell in a shiny curtain across her almond-shaped eyes had become a ball of fluff, and she looked like the before shot for a frizz-reducing serum advertisement.

Built like an Amazon and lacking both pretension and the normal feline tendency toward being aloof, Pye was the ultimate shopkeeper.

She managed to loosen a man's hold on his wallet while making his wife feel like she had just made a new best friend. Of course, that was on a good day. Right now, Clara could tell her hackles were raised and was sure that if she'd been in her feline form, Pye would be nothing but a ball of puffed-out, hissing fur.

An errant thought occurred to Clara, and she whipped around toward mag. "The familiars are getting bored, lacking purpose, and we're in need of some free labor. It's fifteen minutes to closing time and Pye just served the last customer in here. I say we flip the sign, lock the door, and hunt down this vortex. Maggie, you've got to know enough about weather patterns to figure out a tracking solution, right?"

Mag's face lit with inspiration, her eyes darting back and forth as she chewed on her lower lip. She bustled into the back room, throwing a "Hold on" over her shoulder.

"Are you ready for a magical mission?" Clara explained the situation to the two familiars, who had already smelled a plan brewing. They were eager for anything that didn't involve making change or carrying heavy things for demanding humans.

"It's dangerous," She warned, her admonition only making the idea all the more enticing for Pye and Jinx. Which, coincidentally, was exactly what Clara had been hoping for.

"Okay, here's the plan," Clara said. "Mag is going to figure out a way to track this vortex. The two of us will move it to Spurwink Falls, and let 'er rip. Bingo, bango, the water level returns to normal and then we dispel the vortex."

Pyewacket cocked an eyebrow. "And you're going to do that without those pixies noticing? There are hundreds of them. You don't think they've got a few on watch?"

Mag reappeared from the back room carrying a box of supplies. "That's where you two come in. You will be the distractions."

"As if I didn't know you were going to say that after two and a half centuries," Jinx drawled. "Standard procedure, I assume?" He grinned at Mag.

"Pretty much," she huffed, setting the box down on a rustic shaker-style coffee table with a bang.

Hagatha, who they'd nearly forgotten, opened her mouth and let loose what could only be described as a roar, rattling the windows and blowing Clara's shock of chestnut hair into her face. "What about me?" She asked in a tiny voice as if nothing out of the ordinary had occurred.

"Don't think for one second that you're going into the fray." Mag shot her a dirty look, refusing to be ruffled by Hagatha's outburst. "They'll smell you from a mile away, and we'll be attacked by the entire swarm."

Clara sighed. "Actually, Maggie, I think she might be of some help." She ignored Mag's glare, "Maypole trusts you, doesn't she Hagatha?"

"Yeees," Hagatha replied. "You could say that, to some extent."

"Well, you're going to have to exploit it, and I don't want to hear any protests. You got everyone into this mess, including Maypole. It's for her own good. They don't belong here. I don't care how you do it, but take her out of play. Go."

Hagatha thundered out the door—as much as a decrepit old woman with a tennis ball-footed walker could thunder—and disappeared.

Clara brushed her palms together as if wiping off some sort of Hagatha residue. "There, she's out of the way. Now, have you got that contraption worked out yet?"

"Yep, it's all set." Mag held up what looked like an old transistor radio she'd fitted with an additional antenna in the form of a pair of bunny ears from the 1980s. She directed a dollop of magic into her fingertip and turned the dial, causing the antennas to spin wildly. "Let's go."

Pye and Jinx transformed into their cat forms with a shudder and a whoosh, and the foursome trotted out the door and into the VW bus.

"Now," Mag explained, "since there's no engine in the Volkswagen, we'll get less audible interference, and the metal frame will conduct enough energy to amplify the signal. All we have to do is wait for the radio to give us the coordinates, and bada-boom, we've located our vortex. You all know what to do when we find it, right?"

Nodding, Clara pulled out of the driveway while Mag held the equipment in her lap and the familiars meowed their understanding.

An hour later, after they'd circled north by the church in Harmony's town center and past the Riverside Motel, then cut across to where the Rolling Hills Golf Club was located, and finally down along the river adjacent to the Oarhouse Inn, the novelty of the plan had worn off.

"Where in Hades could it be? I know it's not visible, but it's a funnel cloud the size of a tour bus, for crying out loud," Mag grumbled. "I hope Hagatha hasn't tipped off Maypole. It might have been a bad idea to assign her that task."

"Oh, don't worry about that. I slipped a charm into Hagatha's pocket when she wasn't looking. Even if Maypole lands on her shoulder, Hagatha won't be able to see or hear her." Clara grinned. "When Hagatha gets tired of looking, she'll come back. If we ever find this thing, it'll all be over by then."

"Brilliant, Clarie. We could modify that for—" Mag's sentence was cut short by the sound of a foghorn blaring from the transistor radio, then a smooth electronic voice said in a pleasant tone, "In one mile, your destination will be on your left."

Clara raised an eyebrow and looked over at her sister. "You bespelled it to sound like the GPS lady? Why didn't you just use that old GPS unit that's been laying around the back room?"

"Because that uses a different type of signal, Clarie. Besides, you'd drive off a cliff if that woman told you to, so I figured it was my best option. Now stop questioning my methods and just do what she says."

As instructed, Clara continued on ahead, searching the skies for any anomaly that might indicate the exact position of the vortex.

"In thirty-five yards, take a U-turn." The radio intoned. Sighing, Clara kept driving, looking for a shoulder or a turn-off that would allow her to reverse direction.

"I SAID, MAKE A U-TURN!" The GPS lady was annoyed, and the foghorn noise continued to sound every ten seconds or so.

"I can't make a U-turn right here, stop telling me how to live my life!" Clara was beginning to understand why Mag loathed the turn-by-turn instructions feature of her maps app.

Finally, after the VW had crunched and bounced a mile down an old dirt road, a shimmer of magic rose up in front of them, floating just over a field of wild blueberries that had shriveled when the cloud siphoned off all their juice.

"Okay, now!" Mag sent a whoosh of magic to open the back door of the bus and out streaked Pyewacket and Jinx, eager to try their hands—or, more accurately, their paws—at catching a stray honey pixie or two.

A flurry of hissing and meowing followed, and the charm of pixies fluttered into the sky in one dark mass that contrasted against the swirling vortex.

Quick as foxes, Mag and Clara pooled their magic to create a thick, glowing lasso made of witchlight and Balefire. Mag grabbed hold of the end, and whipped the rope around her head in a circular motion, "Go!" She screamed, triggering Clara to conjure enough wind to catch the narrow end of the funnel while the pixies were distracted.

Mag tied the lasso to the rear bumper of the VW, while Clara hopped into the driver's seat and mashed the gas pedal, knowing Pye and Jinx would catch up to them once they'd lured the pixies far enough away for the sisters to complete their task.

What they weren't counting on was the wall of fluttering Faeland creatures guarding the entrance to the falls. Hagatha balanced precariously on top of a flat, three-foot-long rock that jutted over the precipice, her cheeks carrying the cruel marks of a dozen pixie pecks. Maypole fluttered near her shoulder, surrounded by a small swarm of her friends, threatening to topple the ancient witch into the shallow basin below.

"Go ahead and let her fall," Mag hollered from the passenger seat, much to Clara's dismay. "You'd be doing us a favor. Go on, Haggie, this is your swan's song."

"Maggie, what are you thinking?" Clara hissed. "Oh," Realization dawned on her as something in the rear view mirror caught her eye. Mag had used the distraction to give the lasso enough time to uncurl itself from the bumper, and now the vortex was slowly moving toward the river.

"If you've got anything in your bag of tricks that will keep Hagatha from being dashed to bits on the rocks, you'd better pull it out now." Her bad leg forgotten, Mag leaped out and began to pick her way down the path to the base of the falls.

On Mag's heels, Clara rummaged around in her purse for something—anything—useful. This was one of those times to trust the universe and the powers that watched over witches and humans alike because she needed to pull a miracle out of her butt. Well, out of her bag, but at that moment, it felt the same.

When her fingers closed on one of the shop samples, an effervescing bath bomb, she blessed Maggie's penchant for certain types of TV shows.

"Remember the episode of Scorpion where Walter was falling and they had to make the water bubbly so he wouldn't die?"

"Perfect." Yanking up her skirt, Mag revealed the reason why she tended to avoid pants in favor of dresses. Strapped around her thigh, Lara Croft-style, was a wand holster. Mag selected her best elder wand from the three present, and Clara knew she would never get that image out of her head. Once seen, some things are burned on the brain.

The next few seconds passed in a blur. The elder wand danced and swirled as Mag called stones and mud to dam up the river. The water level under the falls rose high enough and Clara tossed the bath bomb. She hit it with an engorgement spell in midair, and when it hit the water, it was the size of a small boulder.

"Goodbye, cruel world." Playing it to the hilt, Hagatha executed a nearly flawless swan dive into the bubbling pool, right before Clara realized the old witch could have just winked out and back in a safe space.

But the drama distracted the pixies long enough for the vortex to seek the biggest source of water, which was the dammed up basin full of effervescing bath bomb bubbles and old witch.

With a mighty roar, the tornado-shaped tail dipped down to siphon up the scented water while Hagatha paddled to the edge of the pool.

"What was in that thing? I feel all tingly." She wiggled her shoulders as she reappeared next to Clara.

"Eucalyptus and spearmint. It's from the cold remedies line, good for clearing the sinuses." To her sister, she said, "What's the plan, Mags?" She pulled out her wand and held it at the ready.

"Well, I was thinking we might need to feed it some Balefire, but I don't think that's going to be necessary. I think your bath bomb gave it indigestion. Look!"

Bubbles pinged around inside the once-transparent vortex creating an increasingly whitened froth that made it look like a huge curl of whipped cream. The more water it drained from the pool, the faster the bubbles expanded until it reached critical mass.

"It's going to—"

It reminded Clara of the scene in Ghostbusters when the marshmallow man exploded. Foam rained down over the waterfall, and over the pixies, who were none too happy to be covered in eucalyptus and spearmint. They flew away in a buzzing cloud of disgust.

It rained down on the bus and the three witches, too.

"Blow." Mag finished with a giggle.

Clara hadn't heard that girlish sound in a hundred years and it nearly brought a tear to her eye, but instead, she let out a chuckle, too.

Pretty soon, all three women were leaning against the side of the bus, too weak from laughing to climb back inside.

That was how Pye and Jinx found them.

"I'm glad you find this so amusing," Scratches and peck marks marred Pye's arms, and there were even a couple on her face. "While you were out here playing"— she looked around to assess the situation—"with bubble bath, we were taking our mission seriously. Just look at Jinx. He's traumatized. Cats are supposed to hunt birds, not be attacked by them."

If Pye meant her lecture to have a sobering effect, it missed the mark as the first drops of much-needed rain plopped into the dry soil and pinged off the van.

Jinx let out a high-pitched eek and dived into the back seat. Like most cats, he despised being wet. Pyewacket followed at a more sedate pace, casting a final glare over her shoulder at her witch companion.

"I can't help but notice Hagatha never asks *her* familiar to do things like this," She slammed the door behind her.

"Better take a detour on the way home, hit the fish market. I think we're going to be having salmon for dinner," Clara said.

"For a week at least," Mag agreed.

# Chapter Nine

"Why is it always feast or famine?" Clara wondered out loud the next morning as the sky rumbled with thunder, and raindrops pelted, unrelenting, against the metal roof of Balms and Bygones.

After a short phone call from Penelope, she was, for once, in a worse mood than her sister. "I'm glad it's raining now, and the race is still a go, but it's so wet that Trek has moved the sets to the municipal building, and we're going to have to hold tonight's coven meeting at Gertrude Granger's house of perpetual Christmas."

Gertrude's obsession with Santa Claus went so far beyond bone deep there was speculation eggnog ran through her veins instead of blood. She dressed like an elf, her house smelled of cookies, and she hoarded Christmas spirit in jars in her basement.

All of those would be easy enough to overlook if not for Jingle Bells playing on an everlasting loop. The woman needed to be considerate of guests and pick another song at least once in a while.

"Look on the bright side," Mag suggested. "We succeeded in our mission, thwarted the pixies, and brought back the rain. That's an accomplishment. And, we might actually get the chance to practice some magic tonight. I don't know why this coven holds meetings that are supposed to be kept secret in a public building, anyway. We get out to the woods only about once a month, and the rest of the time we might as well be solitary practitioners."

"When did you become the optimistic one?" Clara stuck her tongue out at Mag's back. "And I know solitary suits you just fine, but I enjoy the feeling of communal power."

Mag rummaged around in the coat closet and pulled out a fringe-bedecked suede jacket that belonged in a costume shop. Or a museum.

"I never said I didn't, but when there's dissension in the ranks, it's difficult to find common ground." She shrugged the jacket on and took an appraising look in the mirror.

"So, I practice in my own way, and plan to do so until things change." Mag shrugged. "This regime is either going to self-destruct, or we'll find a way to come together. I'll do everything in my power to ensure it's the latter, but I'm not made out of miracles."

"I don't expect you to be, Maggie. It's not all on you." When Clara looked up and saw what her sister was wearing, she frowned. "You're not wearing that in public. Put it back in the closet before it's seared in my memory."

Mag complied, but not before spinning in place just to see the fringe fly.

"Besides, we have other things to think about. All our suspects will be at the municipal building, and it's Sunday, so we don't even have to worry about the shop." Clara put her cell phone inside her purse, pointed a finger at it, and loosed a bolt of magic. The bag wiggled and shrunk into a miniature version of itself, which she pinned to her top. "There, that's what I call hands-free."

With Harmony's town square being only a hop, skip, and jump away from the shop where Mag and Clara both lived and worked, it took less than twenty minutes to get there on foot, even through the wooded trail that ran along the riverbank. But today, with the rain falling in sheets, the VW bus seemed a better option.

Still, with the influx of tourists and the team from Trek, Mag and Clara had to park so far away from the municipal building they were soaked to the bone by the time they crossed the threshold.

A quick trip to the ladies' room and a wink of a drying spell fixed the problem handily. It was such an easy, convenient use of their gifts that Clara wondered again why Penelope thought they should deny themselves. It was a question worth exploring, but not right then.

They'd transformed the meeting room into a makeshift set, with a director's chair arranged behind a pair of studio lights and a bank of monitors for replaying footage lined up against one long wall. Crew weaved around one another, choreographed by routine, setting up workstations and shuffling equipment.

Skip had taken to his new position with an air of inflated importance. Amid the pall that Kevin's death had draped over the staff, he was barking out orders as if he'd been crowned king.

"Ten minutes till cameras roll, people, pick up the pace," he snapped, setting in motion a flurry of activity and several eye rolls.

Jason and Grant stood together against a wall out of the way of foot traffic but close enough to the action to hear what was going on, and watched the proceedings with interest.

"Good, you're here." Matt sidled up next to Mag and Clara, his face unnaturally flushed thanks to the makeup team, who had laid it on thick in an attempt to cover the paleness that had settled there since Kevin's death.

"We need some townsfolk to answer a few questions on camera, and I convinced Skip you two would make for some good local color. Your interview is going to go a little longer than planned." Matt smiled, and Clara wondered who would dare say no to that face. "I hope that's okay."

Mag grimaced, "We've only been living here a few months. I'm not sure we're the right choice."

"You won the flotilla race, and you own a business in town. Seems like you qualify. Besides, I like you more than most of the people in this room. Please?"

Matt looked like a little boy waiting to be told whether or not he could take a cookie from the jar, and when Mag agreed to appear on camera, Clara's suspicions that her sister held a soft spot for the man were confirmed.

"I'll let the crew know, and we'll call you when we're ready," Matt said over his shoulder as he walked away. "Don't go anywhere."

"Matty and Maggie sittin' in a tree," Clara whispered in Mag's ear—payback for the constant comments regarding Mayor McCreery she had to endure every time the man made an appearance.

Mag glared at Clara and stuck out her tongue. "That's not what this is, and you know it."

"Yeah, yeah, but part of me wishes it was. At least I'd know you haven't given up all hope for the entire male population." Clara retorted.

"Pot, this is the kettle. Guess what? You're black again," Mag grumbled and took another look around. "Oh, great. There's Perry Weatherall, and it looks like he's about to give an interview himself. Penelope, too. You know, I don't think they're taking this feud seriously. I've seen them together three separate times now."

"You don't think they're … you know, you?" Clara's stomach churned at the thought. "I like Perry, and I can't imagine what he'd find attractive about her abrasive personality. Then again, since he can't see through her glamour, she probably looks like the prime piece she makes herself out to be."

To the witchy eye, a glamour spell looks like a ghost of double vision laid over the true face underneath, and what was under *that* glamour would be grounds for a false-advertising lawsuit.

"Or she's up to her old tricks again. I swear, Clarie, this whole business about not doing magic in public had to come from somewhere, and I've heard rumblings about someone casting a couple of love spells gone bad. At first, I figured it was Gertrude—she's a cougar if I ever saw one—but now, I'm wondering if it was Penelope. It would explain a lot. Particularly how Perry's tune has changed since the flotilla banquet. He looked embarrassed that night, and now he seems perfectly comfortable."

"I wouldn't be surprised if she was meddling with his heart. Daft witch. Love spells never work the way you want them to." Clara sighed. "Add it to our never-ending list of fires to put out. Come on, let's do a little snooping while we wait for them to call us down." Clara pulled Mag behind her and chose an out-of-the-way spot to eavesdrop.

They settled next to a trio of adjustable partitions that had been arranged in a U-shape with the open end positioned out of view. Clara noticed something moving behind the crack created by two of the corners and squinted to see who was huddled there. "I think that's Grace, Maggie, look." She pointed.

"Here," Mag said, pulling a pair of glasses out of the bag she carried strapped to her waist. "My charms aren't as high-end as yours, but I've turned these into x-ray glasses. Only one charge, but this seems like as good a time as any to test it out."

Clara took them and perched the glasses on the tip of her nose. She smiled and gave Mag a thumbs up, impressed with the clarity of her charm. The partition disappeared, and she could see what was going on behind it.

With curiosity, Clara turned her head and watched as the molecules of each wall seemed to shimmer and shift. "They need to clean the broom closet, and it looks like the front desk clerk is playing Candy Crush while she's supposed to be working. So cool, Maggie."

"Will you please focus," Mag grumbled, covering a smile at Clara's praise.

"Oh, yeah," Clara returned her gaze to where it started and watched Grace for a long moment. It was the closest they'd managed to get to her since the day she'd found Kevin's body.

If she had to pick a single word that best described Grace at that moment, Mag would have gone with hollow. She sat, unmoving, barely blinking, her eyes dead under the mask of makeup, her face so still it looked like wax.

It creeped Mag out and that was saying something.

Clara grappled with whether to approach Grace and initiate a conversation, but by the time she'd come up with an opening line, Skip turned the corner.

"We need you on set. Interviews are about to begin," he informed her without even seeming to notice her appearance. That proved to Clara at least that he cared more about his job than he did his cast's state of mind.

When Grace stepped into the spotlight, her transformation stunned the Balefires into open-mouthed silence. It was as if someone flipped a switch and her corpse had come back to life. The smile ranged from her lips all the way up to sparkling, long-lashed eyes as she flipped her hair back behind one shoulder with an expert toss.

Mag was creeped out all over again.

"I'm ready." The woman was a consummate actress if she could pull off this much animation when the cameras started rolling.

As head of the Harmony's most prominent civic organization, Perry went first and talked up the aspects of the town that would hopefully pull in a few more tourists when the piece aired.

Then it was Mag and Clara's turn. Feeling like a prize fool, Mag explained the inspiration behind their flotilla entry, and Clara answered a few questions about why they'd chosen the town of Harmony, and how they'd come to open Balms and Bygones there. So many people asked why they'd decided to peddle both antiques and a line of personal care products, that Clara felt she'd answered the question a million times.

"We feel like the town has welcomed us with open arms, and we love it here. Hearing new friends cheering us on during the race was a wonderful experience." When Clara turned on the charm, Mag knew their business was going to soar.

"You did great," Matt said as they stepped away from the limelight.

"Grant and Jason, you're up. We'd like to have you two answer questions together since you were a team the year you won." Skip's delivery of the word 'won' carried the fine edge of sarcasm, and Grant's eyes narrowed at the hint of derision.

Grant exchanged a look of irritation with Jason, and snapped at Skip, "Drop the attitude or we're done here. Whatever happened that day, I put my heart and soul into that race and I won't have you belittling me on or off camera. You got that?"

Skip swallowed hard but backed down with a mumbled apology. Typical bully.

Matt, having caught the entire exchange, pulled the pair aside. "Don't let Skip get to you. You won, we lost, and to be perfectly honest with you, if we hadn't, I wouldn't have this job. It was the best thing that's ever happened to me, coming in second place. Everybody won, everyone's happy. At least, everyone was."

The reference to Kevin halted the conversation immediately and he took a deep breath. "Let's just try to move forward. Skip is just a power-mad jerk. Always has been, but now he has actual power and thinks it's his right to lord it over everyone."

"He's right, you know," Grant commented to Jason once Matt had returned his attention to the interview that was just finishing up. Penelope was on screen, her fake eyelashes batting so hard she looked like a butterfly in a windstorm. "We got the endorsement, and we've both done well for ourselves."

"Maybe so," Jason answered, his gaze locked on Matt's face, "But there's a reason why I've avoided this world for the last ten years. I needed to move on, and the last thing I want is the past dredged up again."

Grant nodded in understanding, "Believe me, man, I get it."

Giggling like a teenager, Penelope walked off-set and scanned the room until she found Perry. She made a butt-waggling beeline in his direction and praised his performance with lots of arm patting and more eye batting.

Mag couldn't hold back a snort.

"That's a wrap, folks," Skip said. "We'll review the footage and call you back tomorrow if we need anything additional." He dismissed the group and took a seat in front of the bank of monitors, eager to get to the next phase of his workday.

Holly shot a dirty look at Skip and called for attention. "Just a moment, please. I need you all to see Jane on your way out"—Holly pointed to the intern, who was stationed at the exit—"And give her your signed release forms. We can't use your interviews if we don't have a form. Thank you all again for your time."

"You handle the paperwork, I'm going after Grace." Leaving Mag annoyed at standing in line, Clara sped toward the side exit and arrived in time to see her quarry slide into the back of a black SUV and slam the door just before it pulled away.

"Missed her again." As Clara watched with frustration, another vehicle pulled into the empty space and Lynn Nye, almost unrecognizable in street clothes, got out of the battered old Honda.

"That was Grace just leaving, wasn't it?" Apparently, she'd been ducking Lynn as well.

"It was, but the rest of the cast and crew are inside."

"She's like trying to catch an eel in an oil barrel," Nye observed. "I've got news about the murder weapon and I wanted to ask her some questions, but I can talk to the others first."

"Did you find it? The murder weapon, I mean."

"Not exactly, but we know Kevin Cardiff was killed with one of these." Lynn's hand came out from behind her back and she held aloft a length of red and gold rope.

While she delivered the bombshell, Nye guided Clara back inside and raised her voice so that last sentence echoed through the space and drew the attention of everyone in the room.

"It's one of the drapery ties from the hotel."

Silence fell over the room for a split second, and then the buzz of whispered comments began to circle.

"Someone's worried right about now." Coming up from behind, Mag stated the obvious while the three women watched faces for signs of guilt; instead, they saw nothing but renewed sorrow over the death of a co-worker and friend.

That lasted for about half a second. Right up until the image of Grace and Kevin locked in an embrace flashed across the largest of the monitors mounted on the wall. Someone let out a shocked sound and all eyes turned toward Skip, who had his hand on the controls.

"Oh, sorry. You weren't supposed to see that." Skip's statement was a blatant lie. The smug tone and smirk on his face gave evidence that he meant to play the footage in front of the police. Probably in front of the crew as well, since that would cause the biggest scene.

"You're a total jerk, you know that?" The angry tirade came from an unlikely source, Jane the intern. "And you can fire me for all I care, I don't make any money from this anyway, but I'm going to say what I think of you before I go."

"Janie." Matt's voice held a note of something deeper than simple caution. Admiration, Clara decided, tinged with protectiveness. An odd combination for two people who appeared not to know each other well. "I appreciate your enthusiasm, but I can handle Skipper just fine on my own."

The subtle insult scored a direct hit, and Skip turned surly. Or more surly, since that was his base level and he went up or down from there.

"If you're looking for someone who had a reason to want Kevin dead, there you go." Skip waved a hand to indicate the paused screen with the kissing couple. "Seems his woman was stepping out on him."

Whatever reaction Skip expected, it probably didn't include Matt laughing in his face.

"You really are out of the loop, Skippy my man. Grace and Kevin have been together for quite some time now. There's no scandal here; they had my blessing. I've set my attentions elsewhere." His gaze landed on Holly who, face flushed and eyes snapping with fury, turned on her heel, and left the hall. The slamming door sounded loud in a room gone quiet with surprise.

Mag glanced at her sister with a raised eyebrow, "What was that all about?"

"You got me."

"Well, Clarie. Something tells me we're not getting to that coven meeting tonight after all." Mag didn't seem all that upset at the prospect.

Clara sighed and watched her chance to practice a little communal magic fly right out the window.

# Chapter Ten

Back home, under the night sky, Clara held out a cupped palm, concentrated and called a ball of Balefire to hover just over her skin. Not that the flames would have burned her, anyway. Just one of the perks of being a Balefire witch. Fire that heats but does not burn and feeds the magical soul.

Flipping her hand over, she rippled her fingers to send the ball of fire dancing across the knuckles, flicked it to her other hand and repeated the series. Like a living thing, the flames writhed and played over her skin, faster and more graceful with each turn of her hand.

"You ever get bored, you could make a killing in Vegas with that act." Half joking, Mag snatched the glowing orb and set it hovering a foot off the ground, and expanded it to fire-pit size.

"Playing with fire is restful; it settles my mind and helps me focus."

At the crook of Mag's finger, a pair of lounge chairs reared up on spindly legs and marched across the patio stones to settle invitingly next to the fire. The sisters settled gratefully into the depths of the striped canvas, and Mag kicked off her shoes so she could toast her toes in the Balefire flame.

Moments of peace like this had been rare on the vine the past few days, and she intended to make the most of this time. She'd no more than breathed out a sigh of contentment when a fluffy white cat stalked out of the house and settled on her lap to purr loudly.

When another purr rose from the vicinity of Clara's lap, she assumed Pyewacket had also come out for a cuddle.

For a good ten minutes, Mag banished all thought other than how good the warm flames of her namesake felt on her feet, and how nice it was to run tickling fingers under her familiar's chin while he purred and stretched out long across her lap.

In another minute, she'd have been sound asleep, but Clara broke the silence, pulling Mag back to the grim reality that someone had died and they needed to figure out why.

"It all comes back to motive," she said. "Who stood to benefit from Kevin's death, or was holding a grudge against him? And why kill him now? What was the trigger?"

There would be no nap until they'd hashed out the details, so Mag gave in and started to list the possibilities.

"Skip got an instant promotion, and from what I've seen, didn't harbor any love for Kevin. But, there was no guarantee he'd get the promotion if Kevin was out of the way, and it would have been easier to get the man fired than to kill him. Makes for a flimsy motive. And, to be fair, young Skip doesn't seem to like anyone."

Clara hummed her agreement and added, "I'd say the feeling was mutual. He's not going to win a prize for his people skills. Someone in a Trek jacket followed Kevin down to the pool. Even without that piece of information, I'd have to peg one of the staff. Kevin hadn't been in town long enough to make a mortal enemy."

"Not likely," Mag agreed. "This was too personal. And you'll agree they all had the opportunity, so that still leaves Skip on my list. Plus, it was pretty obvious he showed the footage of that kiss on purpose, and why would he do that?"

"To cast shade on Matt or Grace would be my guess."

"Grace stays on the list, too." The lawn chair creaked as Mag settled herself into a more comfortable position. "First, there was something going on with her at the banquet." She ticked off the reasons on the fingers of her right hand. "Then, we saw her fighting with Kevin on the night he died, and now that we know they were a couple, that puts her in a precarious position. Plus, she's been dodging us ever since she found the body. And there's still the question of what you overheard Matt and Holly discussing during the police interrogations."

"Speaking of which, what about Matt? Did today's revelation put him out of the running?" Clara had her own ideas but waited for Mag to venture an opinion.

It wasn't long in coming. "I can't see any reason for him to want Kevin dead. They were friends, and it doesn't look like Grace came between them. Professionally, Matt's job is in a precarious state because he and Skip don't get along."

"All true," Clara agreed. "He stands to lose more than he gains by Kevin's death. Can't discount him entirely because he could have been holding a grudge, but on the surface, he looks to be in the clear."

"That leaves Holly, Grant, Jason, and that perky little intern. I like her. She's got sass and fire unlike Holly, who strikes me as a cool customer." As an aside, Mag added, "Got any marshmallows in the kitchen? I could go for one right now. And something to drink while you're at it."

"Second shelf in the pantry, behind those organic crackers you hate so much, and if you want a snack, go get them yourself. I'm not waiting on you."

"Crackers are supposed to be light and crispy wafers of flaky goodness, not a box of tree bark masquerading as food. Didn't ask you to go anywhere, either. What kind of witch are you that you can't call a bag of marshmallows from the kitchen? Or is it the personal gain thing again?"

"Shut up, Maggie." A bag of marshmallows dropped onto Mag's lap, and a bottle of Twinkleberry wine accompanied by two glasses popped onto the table. "Half a glass, I don't want to have to carry you to bed."

The faerie-made wine tasted like heaven but packed one hell of a punch.

"You never did." Indignant, Mag defended her honor. "I woke up in the pumpkin patch with my clothes on backward the last time. But I take your point. Half a glass is plenty. Now, where were we?"

"We were about to discuss whether Holly had a motive for Kevin's murder, and again, unless there's a personal connection we haven't found out about, she had more to lose than to gain by his death." Clara took the first sip of the potent wine and felt like the top of her head might fly off.

"What if she and Matt were in cahoots with Skip, and they bumped him off so they could boost the ratings? His death is getting a lot of press. Or Holly had a crush on him and when he said no, she lost it and killed him. Maybe she had a crush on Grace and wanted him out the way so she'd have a shot. Hell, maybe she had a thing for Kevin and was jealous." Mag's imagination took flight. "Or, maybe it was Grant."

"How do you figure?" Grant was the last person on Clara's list, and only on there at all because he had opportunity like everyone else who stayed at the hotel. "I got the impression he and Jason hadn't had a lot of contact with Kevin or Matt in recent years."

"Jealousy? Kevin played Lord Bountiful with the sponsorship for Rockopotamus Canoes, it could have rankled." A ladylike hiccup issued from the vicinity of Mag's chair. "And Kevin was tossing back the booze that night. Maybe he's a mean drunk."

"Not like you, huh Maggie?" After a second of silence, she peered over in Mag's direction. "Maggie?"

The only answer Clara got was a gentle snore.

# Chapter Eleven

With the dill plants Clara enchanted having come nearly to harvest, it was time to banish the pixie pests back to the Faelands, once and for all.

Unfortunately, Hagatha could smell a pickle from a mile away, and had shown up ready and raring to go. "Once they're gone, things should go back to normal immediately. Easy as pie. It's a good thing all you young'uns underestimate me. If it weren't for my brave dive into the falls, you'd never have gotten rid of that vortex, and they'd still be multiplying like bunnies."

"Don't pat yourself on the back too hard. A charm of pixies managed to put one over on you, and you've dragged us into your problems. Sending them back where they belong is going to be a nightmare." Mag's verbal pin popped the bubble of Haggie's pride.

"They're pixies. We're bigger and smarter than them." Not that Hagatha sounded entirely convinced as she poured more growth potion into the soil around Clara's dill plants. The sharp tang coming off the delicate fronds would entice even the most stubborn of male honey pixies.

"I know I am." The insult lacked subtlety, exactly as Mag had intended.

"Upstart," Hagatha sneered.

"Battle-axe," Mag returned.

"Weenie."

"I'm rubber—" Mag started to sing-song, but Clara told her to shut up.

"Just stop sniping at each other," she said. "Though, you have given me an idea, I just need a minute to pull it into focus. Glare at each other if you must, but do it silently."

Turning her back and fully expecting her sister to act like a child, Clara closed her eyes to concentrate and let the thought bloom fully. Rubber. That was the word that had sparked something in Clara's brain.

Sneaking up on the pixie enclosure would be child's play. Using the right charms and spells, the three witches could tap dance naked under the Pixie's hive without being discovered. But neither of those things would hide the process of opening multiple portals to Faerie.

Clara's silencing charms only worked on the bearer and those things he or she came into direct contact with. Portals couldn't be touched, and therefore, couldn't be charmed into silence. Not that the noise was the biggest problem.

A distraction at the right time would obliterate any telltale sound, and Hagatha would know best how to handle that little snag given her study of the creatures. Hiding *multiple* attempts to open a doorway into the right area of the Faelands would take more than a simple distraction.

I'm rubber…the phrase pinged around in her mind again.

Rubber. Things bouncing off rubber. Rubber acting like a mirror.

"I know what we need to do, and it's brilliant if I do say so myself." Without explanation, Clara sailed out the door.

When Mag and Hagatha caught up with her, she was wandering through the herb garden muttering to herself. "Sap, or silver? Needs to be clear, but still get the job done. Quartz points? No, wait."

Oblivious to the fact the others were right behind her, Clara shouted for her sister. "Maggie, do we still have that wheelbarrow full of ulexite?" She spun and nearly ran Hagatha down.

"Oh, sorry. We need to buy some time, right? Maintain the atmosphere inside the enclosure without letting the pixies know we're working against them to reverse the spell. Lull them into a false sense of security. And what better way than to create an illusion we can hide behind?"

Clara whipped the shed doors open, stepped inside, and came back out with three sizable chunks of the stone known for its fiber-optic qualities.

"Ladies, we're going to pull a Hagatha."

**Between** the thump of Mag's cane and the double-thump of Hagatha's walker, the pixies would hear them coming from a mile away. A complication none of them had foreseen, certainly not either of the offending parties. That would have involved admitting a weakness, and the inability to do so was another trait both Mag and Hagatha shared.

"Here." Clara handed Hagatha an old soda-can tab. "It's the silencing charm I told you about." When the older witch shot up an eyebrow, she got defensive. "What? I like to use recycled items. Just give it a rub to activate it, and two quick squeezes to turn it off."

To demonstrate, she pulled an identical tab from her pocket and exaggerating the motion, rubbed a finger across the metal, then hopped up and down while shouting to prove the charm worked. A double-squeeze made her audible again.

"You have yours, Maggie? Hand it over."

Mag spent a few seconds searching through the ugliest fanny pack ever made. Neon green with hot pink piping and spelled to hold any item she needed carrying, Clara wouldn't have been surprised if Mag pulled an elephant out of it.

"Got it," Mag said, handing it over. "Sorry about the pocket lint, I haven't had time for housekeeping lately."

Palming all three tabs, Clara concentrated for a second, then whispered, "Concorporo."

Looking pleased with herself, she started to hand them back. "There, now they're linked. Sort of like an intercom system inside of a bubble of silence. We'll be able to hear each other even in a whisper."

"I don't suppose your bubble of silence could also be used as an umbrella?" Now that the pixies hold on the weather had been broken, the rain clouds seemed intent on making up for lost time, and the town of Harmony was beginning to look a little bedraggled.

"Might make things easier, now that you mention it," Clara whispered another command into her palm and passed the charms through the Balefire. "That should take care of the rain."

"You always did have a way with charms, Clarie." Pride threaded through Mag's voice and the pet name she used for her sister.

"Can we get on with it already?" Hagatha grumbled. Given the choice, she'd have voted for a full-on, frontal attack. But that was Hagatha for you. Formidable as she was in her dotage, she must have been a bundle of firecrackers in her youth. Or, more likely, dynamite.

Under protest, Hagatha supplied the few drops of pixie honey needed to adapt the invisibility potion to hide them only from the tiny creatures and not each other.

"Should we go over the plan one more time?" These days, Mag preferred preparation over inspiration just to be on the safe side.

"We're going." Thunder kicked behind the exasperated order. "Now." Quaffing the invisibility potion and snatching the charm from Clara's hand, Hagatha activated it.

Her outline went fuzzy around the edges to show the spell had worked, and then she winked out, leaving the younger witches no choice but to follow her trajectory to the perimeter of the pixie enclosure.

Drenched and dripping, the forest smelled of fragrant pine, and leaf mold, and pixie. The sweet scent of their honey, a sharp bite of dill, and underlying it all, the musk of pheromones tickling across the skin.

A buzz of angry female pixie voices pitched in discordant harmony whipsawed across Clara's nerves.

"What's going on, Hagatha? Did they see you?" Mag squelched over a patch of mud, feet skating sideways on the slippery surface, and stabbed her cane into the ground for balance.

Inside the enclosure, the honey pixies went about their business as if no one was watching. Their numbers had at least tripled since the last time Mag and Clara visited the compound, and there must've been thousands of the tiny bodies flitting around.

On the slopes of the nearest granite mountain, baby pixies wobbled into their first flights. It would've been enchanting to watch, had the brood not equaled a scourge of epic proportions.

Head cocked sideways, Hagatha studied the activity in the enclosure and listened to the high-pitched swell of dissension. "They're fixing to go to war."

"Against who?" The idea of going into battle lit the old fire in Mag's belly, the one that burned hot and bright when someone needed defending. "And didn't I tell you? Pixie apocalypse. All your fault."

"There ain't going to be no pixie apocalypse. Leastways, not one that concerns the wide world because this is the boys against the girls." She let out a snickering laugh. "Seems like the males figured out they had an ace in the hole."

"If that's a euphemism, it's a really good one." Being both hidden and exposed while they watched the pixies work through a power struggle left Clara feeling like a voyeur, but she couldn't look away. For all the males to decide they had a collective headache tickled her sense of humor.

"If the boys can hold out a little while longer, it works in our favor." Mag placed the last chunk of ulexite in the loose circle arrangement Clara had specified, then stepped back to let Hagatha cast her will upon the stones.

"That's a nice piece of magic," she admitted to the ancient witch when a column-shaped enchantment shot skyward. Only someone who knew to look for it would see the faint shimmer where the two-way mirror effect began.

"Your sister's idea." Hagatha directed her walker through the perimeter of the column and disappeared ahead of Clara. "Is it working?"

"Perfectly. I'll put out the dill and then we'll get going on the portal."

Green and heady, the scent of magically enhanced dill drew the pixie's attention as soon as Mag let the pots hit the ground. She barely had time to clear the area before a cluster of twittering females descended.

"Not very bright are they?" Given the dryness of her tone, it seemed Hagatha's obsession with honey pixies might be coming to an end. One would have thought a dip in the river would have nixed it already, but it seemed the old witch had more of a capacity to forgive and forget than she let on. "S'no wonder they're going extinct if they're this stupid. Pots of dill just appear out of thin air, and they don't give it a second thought."

Like a feathery cloud, the females descended on the dill, stripped the plants to bare stems in seconds and lifted off again.

"Did you see that? They came down like a plague." From behind the image of the empty forest, Clara's voice drifted as Mag made her way toward the barrier.

Once the pixies got their teeth into it, the pungent herb mixed with their saliva to create a musky haze throughout the enclosure. When it penetrated the column where the three witches watched, they all felt the aftereffects.

Grabbing Mag's cane, Hagatha scratched out a crude circle surrounded by a series of runes where the portal should go. "If I'm feeling a little tingle in the loins, the males won't stand a chance."

"One more word about your loins and I'm tossing you through to the Faelands the minute you open the door." An empty threat, but one Mag hoped would shut Hagatha up on the subject. She pulled out the bottle containing the Andruvian flower they'd be using to center in on the mountain regions.

If the coven knew they were opening a door into the Faelands within a mile of town, Penelope Starr would probably lay a polka-dotted egg. Mag would not only pay to see that, but sell tickets. That was one witch who needed to loosen up a little.

"No one's throwing anyone anywhere," Clara said, moving back to give Hagatha room to work. "You know, Maggie, I'm starting to realize the reason you and my daughter never got along when she was young is that you acted too much alike."

The insult hit the mark and Mag's mouth snapped shut while her eyes threatened to burn Clara to cinders. Personally, she thought Clara's daughter was the biggest brat on the face of the planet, with an ego to match, but declined to retort and start a third world war.

With the carping effectively ended, Clara spread a handful of items on a flat rock. It looked like the kind of detritus a mother pulls out of a ten-year-old boy's pockets before throwing his jeans in the wash: two or three glass beads, some bottle caps, a cork, a plastic snake, half a dozen buttons, and a Lego block.

"What's all that?" Curious, Hagatha extended a clawed finger to poke at the debris.

"A few things I thought might come in handy." Clara picked up the buttons, passed through the reflective column, and placed the buttons, three on each side, in two parallel lines leading from the enclosure toward the portal. "These will create a funnel effect to guide the pixies toward the portal."

She named a purpose for each set as she added them to the grid. Charms to keep the pixies calm, some to extend the illusion of the column, but the glass beads were Clara's crowning glory. If they worked, anyway.

"These were a tricky bit of spell crafting," Clara showed the beads to Hagatha. "And I'll need you to donate a few drops of blood to activate the spell, but if it all goes to plan, they'll drain all your magic out of the pixies."

"You mean they'll revert to their true nature?" Even in the middle of a snit, Mag had to ask. "Mating and all?"

"That's the plan."

"Oh, Clarie. I could kiss you." Mag cried, having forgotten she was annoyed with her sister in the first place. "You really are the best of us. You knew I'd sleep easier knowing we haven't sent an altered species to pervert the Faelands."

"Bleeding hearts, the pair of them," Hagatha said to no one in particular. "Strong magic, though." Still, she swiped her ritual knife across her clothes to clean it, and drew it across her palm. The shallow slice welled, and a few drops of scarlet splashed onto the beads of glass.

# Chapter Twelve

Every few minutes, a new wave of dill-scented air spewed out of the pixie enclosure, along with the swell of excited female voices. A quick glance showed the males were trying to hold out, but not without plenty of internal struggle.

Fending off a gaggle of willing females had the boys sweating and shaking with need. One gave in while the three witches finished the final preparations on the doorway, and a shriek of triumph seared the air.

The hormonal spike nearly sent Clara to her knees, and she couldn't help but think how long it had been since she'd needed or wanted a man. But if there'd been one around right then, she might have eaten him whole.

On the other side of the portal, Mag felt a similar rush of tension that burgeoned in her belly and spread like syrup through her veins. Sex was the last thing on her mind though, as the memory of youthful vitality rose up from the depths to become a tangible reality again.

The muscles in her gimpy leg twinged, and firmed. So did a few other parts—ones that had gone south for the winter. For the second time since Hagatha had gotten her into this mess, hope bloomed that she might somehow find a way to turn back the clock.

A hope that needed to be stamped out and fast because Margaret Balefire was a practical witch, and one well-versed in the hard knocks of life. Chasing her lost youth could only end in heartbreak, and therefore, she would not take the first running step.

But she would enjoy walking easily for as long as it lasted. Surely that small mercy could be savored, so Mag tossed her cane aside.

"Looks like it's go-time." Mag dusted off her hands and surveyed the fruits of their labors.

Intricate lines carved into the soil carried all the protection the three witches could summon. Faerie runes mixed with their own familiar sigils served to anchor the doorway between two worlds. Finally, Mag tipped a few drops of Andruvian nectar into the thirsty soil. Hagatha contributed a smear of pixie honey, and Clara added the last piece of magic.

Her eyes burned with inner light while Clara called the sacred fire into her palm, cupped it gently, and slipped the flame into the grooves where it ran like water. Wind-licked tongues flickered and built in a thundering roar to shoot skyward, then fall like a molten curtain, revealing an open doorway to the land of the Fae.

Once the fire-teased spots faded enough for Mag to focus, her mouth dropped open, then she shouted, "Nope. Close it!"

As one, the Balefires shot into action. Clara recalled the life-giving fire, and Mag grabbed a stick to scratch a sigil into the soil. With a whoosh and a bang, the portal fell shut.

"Did you just use the not sign to close that portal?" Breathing hard, Clara checked, and sure enough, there was the familiar circle with a diagonal line through it.

"What's the problem? It worked, didn't it?"

"You could have gotten us killed." Clara admonished.

"Me? I'm not the one who tuned the stupid thing to the palace of the ice queen. Sweet Circe in suspenders, Hagatha. What were you thinking?" Hands shaking, heart still galloping, Mag turned to the old witch who, for once in her long, long life, couldn't rustle up a snappy comeback.

Eyes wide in her pale face, Hagatha circled the charred inscription until she found her mistake. "I put an extra loop here. Hand me that little elder broom and I'll fix it."

Once the offending section of the pattern had been repaired and the rest of the sigils checked for accuracy, it was time to try again.

"Are we ready?" Mag took a deep breath and let drops of nectar fall a second time. Hagatha did her thing with the honey, and Clara summoned a ball of Balefire, though she hesitated a moment before activating the seal.

"Here goes nothing," she shielded her eyes and let the flame fall.

When the whoosh and roar died back, the three witches chanced a peek through slitted lids. Mag's sigh of relief gusted through the clearing when the opening revealed the bucolic scene of a mountainside and not the throne room of an angry Fae queen.

"Let's get this party started." Gathering a few of her bottlecap charms, Clara blew on them and tossed them into the space between the pixie enclosure and the doorway to the Andruvian mountains.

"Fan charms." She answered Mag and Hagatha's unspoken question, then stepped out from behind the mirrored column to direct the flow of air. "If there are any interested males on the other side, the scent ought to bring them running."

The heady mix of dill and pheromones flowed along the air currents, and oddly, turned a misty blue when it melded with the mountain atmosphere. Experimenting, Clara pulsed the fan magic and created a series of puffball clouds that sailed off in a straight line.

"Too high," Hagatha determined and made for one of the scattered charms. The breeze nearly blew her over, but she managed to get control of the magic wind after a short struggle, and, moving closer to the portal, sent the next bits of blue mist scudding closer to the hilltop.

Mag followed suit and soon had clouds bobbing off in all directions. "That ought to do it. And now we wait."

Long moments passed while skies tinged with lavender and palest gold remained barren of any sign of interested male pixies.

"It's not working." If Mag's arms were tiring from the strain of directing the breeze, Hagatha's must be nearly spent, but the old witch stood firm, her arm muscles like tightened cords.

"Give it another minute," she said. "They're coming, I know it."

"You don't know, the sect could have evolved far enough toward being vegetable-based that the sexy female vibes won't work on them. Anything's possible in the Faelands." Clara observed.

"Unicorn feathers!" Hagatha pronounced. "They're males, they smell hormonal females, they're going to check it out. They won't be able to help theirselves."

"Themselves," Mag corrected without thinking.

"Mind your elders, little Balefire."

"Will the two of you please shut up?" Under the bickering, Clara heard something. Not the buzz of wings from the Fae side of the portal, but an excited humming from the females. Either another of their current male harem had finally submitted, or the pixies behind the enclosure sensed new blood.

"I think we might have overestimated our need for the Andruvian males to actually be interested in mating." The humming increased in volume and intensity. "As long as the females think there's a possibility, this will work."

The first buzz of pixie wings sounded from the Fae side of the doorway. An answering hum went up from the females.

"It's time. Drop the spell, Haggie. Quickly." Mag's hormones went into overdrive, and so did the surge of energy. She hadn't felt his good in a long time. "Get ready, Clarie, I think we're going to want to…"

"Duck!" Despite her age, Hagatha dropped like lightning when the spell surrounding the portal fell.

Thousands of wings shook the air as the females dropped the enclosure barrier, and arrowed toward the ascetic pixies whose curiosity had drawn them to the source of the pheromone-laced, dill-scented clouds.

Exhausted males gathered those too young to fly, trussed them into safety nets made from bits of spider web, and followed along behind. The whole exodus lasted no more than two minutes and as the last of the males cast a guarded look over his shoulder, Mag moved to throw dirt over the portal runes and let it close behind him.

That was when Hagatha made her move. Just before the portal slammed shut, Mag watched her roll over the edge to disappear into the Faelands.

"Well, that was something," Clara's understatement fell into the sudden quiet only broken by the steady drip of rain. "Did it work? The nullification spell?" She turned to Hagatha, who should have been able to sense the return of her stolen power. "Where did she go?"

Mag sucked back the whoop she'd been about to release and loosed a few choice words instead. Once the bout of swearing ended, she said, "She crossed over."

"Hagatha died?" Clara misunderstood.

"No, she went through the portal, and now we have to open it back up and go after her." Disgust colored every word.

"I don't think we can. Did you memorize the runes she used? They're already fading, and I, for one, have no interest in spending a thousand years in the winter queen's dungeon."

"That's cold, Clarie. When did you become so ruthless?"

"Maybe it was the day I tried to bind my daughter's magic and we nearly killed each other. Or it could have happened during the years I spent locked in stone as punishment. Or maybe you've rubbed off on me." Clipped tones might have been misconstrued by anyone who didn't know Clara well, but Mag was not fooled. Leaving Hagatha in the Faelands would weigh on both their minds, but she saw no alternative.

If there was one good thing about the day, they'd stopped the rampant reproduction of honey pixies and kept the creatures from taking over the world. Mag figured the thousands of new females they had released back into the wild would be enough to turn the tide against the decimation of the species. If Hagatha were there, she'd have to be satisfied with those results.

Moreover, the loss of the old witch had been no accident. Hagatha had gone through the portal under her own steam and left the sisters behind to clean up yet another of her messes.

Running an assessing eye over the deserted oasis, the other positive thing Mag could see was that the pixies had left their honey-filled hives behind.

# Chapter Thirteen

"If we hurry, we can get down to the pavilion before shooting gets underway for the day," Mag said. "Give me one of those umbrella charms, and we'll take the riverside path. It'll be faster if we don't have to circle town for an hour looking for a parking space."

Mag pointed downstream, and continued on past the shop's backyard, hoping to kill two birds with one stone and scout for some of the berries that grew between the riverbank and woods that ran along behind town.

"Drop one of those charms in the blackberry thicket, and if it's dry enough on the way back we can pick a quart or so. I have a hankering for pie."

Clara nodded. The thought of flaky, buttery crust and juicy, tart berries made her mouth water, "Sounds good to me." She handed Mag an enchanted Barbie shoe and met the raised eyebrow with a challenging stare. Using whatever came to hand was Clara's way of practicing mindful magic.

Their feet quickly ate the distance between Balms and Bygones and the boat launch-adjacent Spurwink Park where the flotilla had taken place. It had only been a week since Mag and Clara's victory, but with all the excitement surrounding the murder of Kevin Cardiff, it seemed a lifetime ago.

The pressure was on to find Kevin's killer before Sunday when, with the canoe race ended, the cast and crew would be ready to move on, leaving Harmony stained by murder and not enough evidence to solve the case.

Unless Matt was willing to share some inside info. He was, Mag and Clara agreed, the most likely person to talk to them honestly about Skip and Holly's possible involvement.

As the pair rounded the last bend in the trail, they could make out a canoe floating in the center of the river, moored by a long rope attached to the dock. With each swell of the current, the boat rocked back and forth, and the closer they got, the clearer it became that the craft was listing to one side.

"There's something in that boat. It looks like it's about to capsize. Think we ought to try to pull it to shore?" Clara asked.

Mag took a look around, "If the crew is here already, they're in the tent staying dry, and that's up beyond that knoll. We're clear." She closed her eyes and concentrated her will toward the canoe. With Clara's assistance, it began to move slowly toward the dock.

"Oh my Goddess," Clara breathed, her tone rife with distress "Maggie, look." Mag's eyes immediately snapped open, the boat continued to drift toward shore, and as it dipped to the side, Mag could see what had raised Clara's hackles.

Matthew Chase sprawled on his back on the floor of the canoe. Water, stained pink with the blood still seeping from his head, washed shimmered around the loose fingers holding the pistol used to start the flotilla. Looking at his ghost-white face, Clara felt her heart try to leap into her throat and drop to her feet at the same time.

"Is he dead?" Mag's eyes frosted over with the first genuine tears Clara had seen since she'd been released from her stone prison the summer prior. There was a reason Mag didn't get attached to mortals, and Clara could tell her sister was sorely regretting giving in to her emotions.

"I don't know." For once, Clara didn't care if someone saw. She blinked from the dock to the canoe, knelt next to Matt, and felt for a pulse. Mag might be used to blood and death in her former line of work, but Clara's heart broke at the sight of his pale face and the scarlet-tinted water.

Under hopeful fingers came the tiniest of flutters.

"He's alive. Barely. I'm going to do what I can for him, you call for help." She fished her phone from her bag and tossed it to Mag, who caught it like it was an annoyed porcupine.

"I don't know how."

"Just touch the phone icon, and then hit 9-1-1. You've seen me use it enough times. It's for Matt."

And for the man who had touched Mag's heart, she figured it out.

"They're on their way. Shouldn't be long."

"It's bad, Maggie. I don't know if he's going to make it." Nonetheless, Clara opened a channel to all the healing magic she could muster and sent it toward the man who lay still as death under her hands. "Hang on, Matt. Just hang on."

With all the magical power at her disposal, Clara could only give Matt as much healing energy as his soul would accept. If he truly wanted to die, nothing would save him.

"Live. Please live."

Maybe her words got through to him, or maybe it was the prayer she directed toward the universe, but she felt another flutter and it gave her hope.

It seemed like forever before the sound of sirens broke over the rush of the river and the hiss of light rain, and longer still before a paramedic stepped into the canoe and nudged Clara aside.

"He barely has a pulse."

"We'll take it from here." Busy hands replaced Clara's and more helped her onto the dock, where she stood next to Mag and watched heroes try to save Matt's life.

Another tear tracked down Mag's cheek, then as quickly as they'd begun, the waterworks ceased and were replaced with the fire of retribution.

"Come on," she said with a growl. "Let's go find Deputy Nye. And then we're going to find the murdering lowlife who did this and make him pay." Mag's icy tone didn't bode well for the culprit; when the elder Balefire set her sights on a target, she never missed.

Following behind, Clara tried to bat away an unpleasant thought she hated to share with her grieving sister.

"Maggie," Clara said tentatively, "It looked like an attempt at suicide." There hadn't been a lot of time to get the full picture, but in the quick glance she'd had, she hadn't missed the small pistol clutched in Matt's right hand. The same side as the bloody wound in his head.

"No," Mag said, shaking her head, adamant. "I don't believe it. I won't."

"He could have killed Kevin, and then felt remorse."

Mag grimaced and slowed. "I suppose. Maybe. Or he was just another victim and this was staged to make him look guilty. Did you ever think of that?"

The futility of the situation sent Mag's temper into a tizzy, and she lashed out at the most convenient target. Wild magic built and lodged in the back of Clara's throat with the kind of hum that set her back teeth vibrating.

"Dial back on the magics, right now." Rubbing her arms to get rid of the prickling sensation and the gooseflesh, Clara hissed the order as police sirens alerted the sisters to Deputy Nye's arrival, and the ambulance pulled away.

The commotion had drawn a crowd of Trek employees to gather just out of sight of the dock. Raised voices expressed concern and worry, but none dared disobey the deputy's order to stay clear.

"You two. I should have known." Nye delivered the statement gently, having picked up on Mag's sour mood and noticed the red rings around Clara's eyes. "Did you have a connection to the victim?"

"Not really. We met him at the flotilla banquet. We were on our way to the shoot," Clara explained, retracing their steps minus the part where they had used magic to pull the canoe to shore. "I'm afraid we contaminated the scene."

"Thanks for that small favor, but you may have saved his life, so I'll let it slide. Tell me what happened."

During the recitation, Mag stepped back and let Clara do the talking. She ran through the series of events, described finding Matt and the gun.

"I won't lie. First responders said it doesn't look good, but if he makes it to the hospital, he'll be going into surgery. I'll give you an update as soon as I know something."

"Are you treating this like an attempted suicide?" Mag spoke for the first time. "Or are you as good a cop as I think you are and not discounting the possibility someone tried to kill a decent man?"

"Let me get a look at the scene and then go to the hospital and see what there is to learn. I'll promise to keep an open mind. That's the best I can offer." Nye dismissed Mag and Clara, then turned her attention to gathering what evidence there was to be found.

"If I'm right, this wasn't a crime of passion or convenience. No one carries a starter pistol around with them. Plus, don't those shoot blanks?" Mag asked as she and Clara made their way up the embankment.

"Still deadly. The gunpowder is sealed in with either plastic or paper which, at close range, can cause damage."

"When did you look that up? I'm still carrying your phone." Pulling it out of her pocket, Mag passed the offending item back to Clara.

"Didn't need to look it up." She heaved a sigh. "Jon-Erik Hexum, one of my favorite actors, died that way."

In a testament to her fondness for Matt, Mag ignored a prime teasing opportunity. "From a wad of paper shot out of a little gun?" Normal humans were more fragile than witches if that kind of thing could kill them so handily.

"No, not exactly. The concussive force caused a blunt-trauma situation and fragmented his skull. Such a beautiful soul, gone in an instant." The second sigh did it, though, and Mag tried to work up a scathing comment.

"If you're so dead set against this being a suicide attempt, what's your alternate theory?" Clara nipped the nastiness in the bud.

"I don't like this one any better, but the only thing that comes to mind is retaliation for killing Kevin." If there was a third option, Mag wished she could dredge it up, because this one meant Matt was a killer and that didn't sit well with her, either.

"I thought the same thing, and if it's retaliation, there's only one person who stands out as a possible suspect. Kevin's girlfriend, Grace. Conveniently, the one person we haven't been able to get close to." Clara lamented.

"What happened?" Jason Trumbell approached Mag and Clara, his yellow slicker flapping behind him, with concern in his bright blue eyes. Grant, huddled against the rain, trailed behind him, peering over the hill toward where Lynn and her team of uniforms examined the contents of the canoe. He wasn't the only one, as the natural inclination to get a peek at tragedy had struck the entire group.

Mag shook her head sadly and pulled the pair off to the side for propriety's sake as well as to get under the canopy of leaves and out of the worst of the rain, "It looks like Matt Chase tried to kill himself this morning. He survived, but it doesn't look good."

Grant's eyes widened to the size of dinner plates and Jason paled, "Matt? I can't believe this."

"Neither can I," Grant said. "And I have to say, this is turning into more of an adventure than I expected. I have a family at home, and my wife is going to insist I return before something else happens."

Clara turned her attention to Grant with interest. "What do you think is going to happen?" She asked.

"I, well, I don't know. It's just, Matt and Kevin had history with this race, and so do I. Jason, too. I'm beginning to think the whole thing is cursed or something," Grant hedged, his gaze flicking to Jason.

Jason clapped him on the back. "You always were superstitious. You never know what's going on behind the public mask, and—" Jason stopped short, a look of understanding crossing his face. "I need to talk to the police. You said it happened this morning?"

"Yes, not too long ago, or we would have been too late," Mag answered without mincing words.

Jason's eyes flicked between Mag and Clara, Grant, and Deputy Nye, who was just cresting the hill.

The Balefire sisters followed behind Jason as he approached the officer, "I may have some pertinent information. May I speak to you in private?" he asked.

"Of course, follow me." Deputy Nye's cheeks pinked, securing the theory she was sweet on the man.

Nye led Jason away from the crowd, toward the squad car she'd parked on the periphery of the chaos created by the television crew's interrupted activities.

Mag grabbed Clara's arm and pulled her in the opposite direction while Grant stared after Jason with a look of concern on his face.

"Ouch, Maggie. Jeez, you just about pulled my arm out of the socket," Clara said, jerking her arm away and rubbing it.

"Shush, Clarie." They circled around a dense pine tree and angled toward where Jason and the deputy were conversing. "Do you still have that pair of headphones?"

Clara removed the bauble that had once been her purse and shook it a few times. With each jostle, the bag got a little bit bigger until it had returned to its normal size. "Here you go."

Mag inserted one earbud and handed the other to Clara, then listened intently.

"Grace Abbott, you say?" Deputy Nye's voice carried a slight lilt that under any other circumstances might have come off as flirtatiousness. In this case, Clara sincerely hoped it was nerves. This was not the meet-cute most women dreamed about, and if the good deputy was going to get distracted from an investigation the second an attractive man turned up, she wasn't going to be nearly as successful as Clara had anticipated.

"Yes, Grace. We were all at the inn last night. The Trek crew was discussing today's shooting schedule, and after a few drinks, the conversation turned to Kevin's death." Jason's tone held only anxiousness and no trace of a reciprocal attraction to the deputy.

"They reminisced for a bit, told a few outrageous stories of things he'd done, but then when Grace entered the room, it turned awkward, and the party disbanded. There was a lull in the weather, so I went out onto the patio to finish my drink, and saw Grace and Matt talking."

"I'm not sure what that has to do with anything." Nye's voice settled into its normal rhythm and cadence.

"Whatever they talked about, it must have been good news because Matt seemed fine when he passed me to go back inside."

Deputy Nye was silent for a long moment, "What time was that?" Nye asked.

"I'm not sure, but it was pretty late. It was close to midnight when I went to bed, so sometime after eleven, anyway."

"And that was the last time you saw Matthew Chase alive?"

Jason considered, then answered. "No, and that's why I wanted to talk to you. The room across from mine is one they're using for storage. Wardrobe, boxes of promotional items, the trophies—those types of things."

"Is that where they keep the starter pistol?" Now Lynn sounded interested.

"Maybe. I only got a glimpse in there once or twice, but anyway, Matt was locking the door behind him when I came out to get the morning paper. He didn't look happy, and when I said hello, or good morning, I can't remember which, he brushed me off, and walked away."

When Nye started to take him through the whole thing again, Mag pulled out the earbud. "I've heard enough. You coming?" Without waiting for an answer, she stomped toward the fork in the trail.

# Chapter Fourteen

"This turns our entire investigation on its ear. Matt being attacked opens up more possibilities than it closes." Mag dared her sister to disagree with the assessment. "And now we've lost our chance to talk to him about other suspects."

"Do you want to take the river trail the rest of the way home? We can grab the van and go to the hospital." Mag answered with a grimace and a nod.

"I hate that place. It smells of chemicals and hopelessness."

"Babies are born there, too," Clara said, glancing at her out of the corner of her eye.

The sentiment fell on deaf ears as Mag shifted gears and fell into the space between alternately muttering out loud and listening to her internal dialog.

She kept her senses open the whole way, but the section of woods between the Oarhouse and the pavilion had turned into a thruway since the team from Trek arrived, and all her witchy intuition could pick up was that a bevy of emotions had played out along the trail.

Clara sighed as the inn's tower loomed into view ahead. "I think once all the excitement has died down and the Trek team has checked out, the river trail might need to undergo a cleansing ritual. Bad mojo everywhere. It practically stinks."

"I know, Clarie. I hope the pixies didn't wipe out all the sage because it's going to take a truckload." Mag's attention zeroed in on something up ahead, and she quickened her pace.

Clara followed behind and heard the muffled sounds of someone crying before she caught sight of the girl. Drenched to the bone, Jane sat on a moss-covered log, head in her hands, her shoulders heaving with sobs.

Mag looked pointedly at Clara and back at the girl, a gesture Clara understood to mean 'tag, you're it'.

"Jane, are you all right?" Clara asked, rolling her eyes at the triteness of the unnecessary question. Clearly, this was a person in distress.

"No, I'm not all right!" Jane wailed, lifting her head to expose a face streaked with mascara.

Clara reached into her purse and fished around until she'd found what she was looking for—a packet of makeup-removing wipes she'd been experimenting with for the personal care line she sold at Balms and Bygones.

The girl let Clara get her cleaned up as if it were the most natural thing in the world to allow a stranger to scrub her face. Clara figured she was either too distraught to care, or she'd gotten so used to the hair and makeup team, it seemed like second nature.

"I know what's happened here is terribly distressing, but you'll get past it, eventually." Clara soothed.

Jane's eyes met Clara's, misery evident in their depths. *Quite a lovely face, funny I never noticed before,* Clara thought to herself.

"You don't understand. They took him away and I'm stuck here worrying because—" Janie clapped her lips closed, and Clara could tell Mag was rapidly reaching the edge of her patience.

"Are you talking about Matt?" Mag barked, earning herself a quelling look from her sister.

Jane attempted to regain her composure by taking a few quivering breaths. "Of course I'm talking about Matt. My husband just left in an ambulance and there's a non-disclosure clause in my contract that means I can't go with him or the press might find out our dirty secret."

Mag sucked in a breath. "Let me get this straight," she said, ignoring Clara completely. "You are married to Matt Chase. *You* and Matt are married?"

Jane looked directly at Mag for the first time and showed a level of composure neither Balefire had thought her capable of, given the state they'd found her in and the brief encounters they'd had previously.

Under the eager-to-please exterior lurked a bit of fire.

"We started dating right after I took this internship about six months ago. It happened so fast, but when it's right, you just know." Jane heaved in another quavering breath and swallowed hard.

"We got married in Hawaii while the show was on hiatus," she continued. "I can show you the license if you don't believe me. Of course, we couldn't tell the cast and crew, what with the whole Matt-and-Grace farce in full swing."

The wheels in Mag's head spun like a turbine for a split second. In her mind's eye, she could clearly visualize a table, and on that table lay the interlocking pieces of a puzzle representing both crimes. Several of the jagged edges hung together, a few here and a few there, and as Mag considered what Jane was saying, a bit more of the picture fell into place.

"Then what are you doing here?" It always boggled Clara's mind that Mag was able to turn her empathy on and off like a garden hose, and come across as sweet as whipped cream when she felt like it. "You can't tell me a piece of paper is stopping you from being with your husband when he needs you."

Or she could turn acid as vinegar.

"No. I'm not. Not anymore." Jane's spine straightened, and she made to leave.

Before you go, I need you to be honest about something. Was Matt with you when Kevin was killed?" Mag minced no words but left no room for Jane to think she was being insensitive.

The younger woman's eyes widened and she nodded, "Yes, he was. And if it had come down to it—if he'd been seriously considered a suspect, we would have come clean and dealt with Holly's wrath."

"Holly?" Mag asked sharply. "She knew?"

"Holly knows everything that goes on with the cast and crew. It's a running joke she has us all bugged."

Clara nodded in understanding. "She's the public relations rep, after all. Clearly, she wanted Matt and Jane's relationship to remain under wraps so she could continue to exploit the cutsie-poo image of Grace and Matt. Something has always seemed off to me, but I couldn't put my finger on it. Now it all makes sense."

"You don't think Holly might have had something to do with Kevin's death do you?" Jane's voice went steely.

Mag raised an eyebrow at the question, "Do *you* think she could have?"

Jane thought for a moment, her eyes darting back and forth as she mulled over the implication. "She's a pitbull, yes. Sometimes it seems like she doesn't have a heart, but I've seen her take care of Grace with more emotion than I'd expect from someone who's just doing a job."

Restless fingers picked at bits of dirt clinging to her pants while Jane continued to consider the question.

"But Holly and Kevin loathed one another, and I know he tried to get her fired last year. If Matty doesn't make it," Jane shuddered, "well, I'm guessing that would be the end of the show, and that's definitely not something Holly would want."

"Does anyone else know about you and Matt being married?" Clara asked.

"The only people we told were Holly and Kevin. It killed Kevin to keep the secret from Grace, but Matt played the 'best buds' card and he caved."

"And that's all?" Mag prodded.

"I think Skip suspects something. You two were on the set the other day. He obviously knew about Grace and Kevin. I don't believe for a second he played that footage of them kissing by accident. I don't understand what his end game would be, though."

Clara and Mag exchanged a look, and Mag gave a slight shake of her head to indicate it wasn't the time to let their own ideas be known.

"Is there anyone we can call for you? You shouldn't be alone at a time like this." Settling onto the soggy moss, and ignoring the dampness seeping along her backside, Clara pulled Janie in for a comforting hug. "We'll walk back to the hotel and make sure you get to the hospital." Her heart went out to the young girl who seemed so lost and alone.

"I'll call my mom from the hospital." Fresh tears welled up and spilled over. "What will I do if he doesn't make it? This wasn't supposed to happen. We were just starting our life together, and now it could be over."

"You need to tell Deputy Nye everything you've just told us." Stepping away for a moment, Clara used her phone to set things in motion.

"I hate to ask, but do you have any idea if your husband might have wanted to kill himself?" Guiding Jane gently toward the hotel, Mag asked the probing question with as much tact as she could muster.

"No. And I know everyone says that at a time like this because they can't bear to think someone they loved was feeling so desperate, but it's true." Jane showed wisdom beyond her years.

"On screen, Matty came across as exactly who he was. A genuinely happy person. I've never known anyone less likely to commit suicide, and I don't believe for a minute it he did this to himself."

"Nothing happened last night or this morning that might have affected his state of mind?" According to Jason, something had.

"He spoke to Grace last night, and I can assure you the news from her was good for us. When he left the room this morning to look for Holly and Skip, he was in a great mood, and even if he wasn't, I'm telling you, he would never take his own life."

Mag picked up on the most important thing Jane had said, "Why was he looking for Holly and Skip?"

"I assumed it had something to do with the shooting schedule for the day, but maybe there was more to it than that." Jane looked overwhelmed at the possibility. "Grace might know, but she's locked herself in her room and will only come out when she has to be on camera."

As they stepped out of the path onto the damp, grassy verge, Mag scanned every face looking for Holly. Clara could handle getting Jane a ride to the hospital, but Mag wanted a word with the cold-hearted PR rep.

Her preference of words would have been one that turned Holly into the slug she deserved to be, but Mag would settle for an old-fashioned tongue lashing.

Keeping Jane from her own husband went beyond the pale.

"Your ride is ready." Clara led Jane to where Lynn Nye was pacing, impatience with what had been, to her, a cryptic phone call and an order to make herself available.

She gave Clara her best who-do-you-think-you-are face and started to ask the question outright, but never got past the who.

"This is Jane and she has information for you that you are going to want to hear. She's Matthew's wife and needs to be with her husband. If you'd be so kind as to get her to the hospital, she can tell you the whole story on the way."

Without waiting for Lynn to agree, Clara helped Jane into the front seat of the car, and practically forced Lynn into the driver's side. "Hurry, please."

"And now," she turned back to Mag, "it's time to talk to Grace. We need to have all the information before we point the finger at Holly or Skip."

# Chapter Fifteen

"The only good thing about this is that we get to engage in a little subterfuge," Mag commented, her spirits somewhat lifted. "Now, hold still." She pointed a finger at Clara, who ducked for cover with lightning-fast reflexes.

"At least use a wand, you old coot. Glamour requires precision when you're performing it on another person." Clara admonished. "On second thought, keep your wand away from me. I'll cast it myself."

Mag rolled her eyes, "First of all, I'm aware of how to perform a simple illusion spell, and second of all, we only have to look like Oarhouse maids. It's not like you have to pass for Christy Turlington. Oh, wait, you already can." In a second infantile gesture, Mag stuck her tongue out at her sister and turned her wand hand on herself.

When the twin puffs of smoke cleared, both Balefires were clad in perfect imitations of the Oarhouse cleaning staff's uniforms, complete with white lapels and matching crepe-soled shoes.

Tilting her head to the side, Clara declared, "It's missing something." She considered a few seconds longer, then flicked a finger at Mag, who suddenly found herself carrying a rainbow-hued feather duster. "That's better."

Not to be outdone, Mag retaliated with an over-sized toilet brush and then found herself wearing a frilly cap. Clara got the matching apron, and her pale blue dress slithered and tightened to show legs encased in fishnet stockings.

"You had to go there, didn't you?"

Flares of magic lit up the poolside changing room, empty now because the rain kept everyone indoors until both sisters had run the gamut of maid uniforms including a cartoon version right out of a Disney movie.

"Truce," Giggling at the sight of Mag in a do-rag, Clara called off the good-natured warfare. "This isn't getting us anywhere and Matthew needs us."

The mention of his name was all it took to turn Mag's face sober again, and in a blink, she was back to the original look. "Let's go."

Keeping their faces averted whenever they ran into any of the real staff, Mag managed to snag a master key card off a cleaning cart.

"Housekeeping." She sing-songed, and knocked on the door three times in rapid succession. Without waiting for permission, she used the card and walked into Grace's room.

Dark behind closed drapes, and cluttered with almost a week's worth of room service debris, the place looked like the cave of an angry bear. Smelled like it, too. How could anyone live like this?

"Get out. I didn't give permission for you to come in." Grace's voice sounded flat and emotionless.

"I'm sorry, but I don't remember asking," Mag replied, cool to the point of icy.

"I know you two! You're not housekeeping. You're the two women from Balms and Bygones. Clara and Margaret, though I think you go by Mag. You won the flotilla race."

For someone who had been described as both fragile and dimwitted, Grace had a memory to rival an elephant's. "What are you doing here? Looking for an autograph? I'm not in the mood."

"We're not here for an autograph, Grace. We're here about Kevin's murder, and about what happened with Matthew this morning." Mag blurted rather rudely. She felt her tone justified, considering she'd just been accused of being a Trek Network groupie.

"I'm not giving interviews either. This isn't just my job, you know. It's also my life." As though she hadn't understood what Mag said, Grace stalked to the door, yanked on the knob, and held it open expectantly. "Please leave me alone."

"Close the door," Clara began softly, for once not irritated at having to play the good cop. "We're not here for an interview, but we did come for information. We're trying to find out who killed your boyfriend, and bring him or her to justice."

"And we're going to find out what happened to Matt." Circling around, Mag carefully pulled the door from Grace's hand and snugged it shut.

Grace appeared surprised, and then doubtful as her widened eyes turned into a frown, "You two are going to solve the case? Who are you, Miss Marple and a grown-up Nancy Drew?"

But she did click on the overhead lights, proving the room was in worse shape than they'd thought, and move into the middle of the space.

"Something like that," Clara smirked. "We've got the mayor's blessing to investigate if it makes you feel any better. What could it hurt?"

Mag, impatient, interrupted, "It's not as though we're accusing *you*, so doesn't that buy us at least a little bit of your trust?"

Grace considered both women's statements and collapsed onto the rumpled bed. "What do you want to know? Actually, why don't you start by telling me what *you* know? Did you say something happened to Matt?"

Watching Grace's reaction closely, Clara dropped the bomb.

"He attempted to take his own life just a little while ago."

The initial shock registered, then was wiped away by something less easily defined.

"No. Not Matt. He's not the type, and I know that's what everyone says," Grace mirrored Jane's opinion, "But he's not. He had everything to live for."

"You mean your relationship," Mag might as well have made air quotes around the word, "and his career."

"Yes, of course." The words had a hollow ring. "You said attempted, does that mean he didn't …" She trailed off as if saying the word die was too painful to contemplate.

"He's in surgery, but it doesn't look good. We figured out the truth about you and Kevin, and Janie told us about her marriage to Matt, so you can drop the act and speak plainly."

The sisters took a seat on a settee at the foot of the bed and delivered a brief account of their investigation so far.

"Well, you're more observant than I would have given you credit for. The whole charade took a toll on me. I loved Kevin, and I was tired of faking it on camera. Actually, on camera would have been one thing, but when Holly insisted that we keep our relationship a secret in our personal lives, I stopped giving a damn about the show."

"How did Kevin feel about the situation?" Unable to help herself, Clara rose to move around the room, putting things to rights. Something about piles of dirty dishes and empty wrappers made her fingers itch.

"It was different for him, being the producer and director. He felt like everyone's job was on his shoulders, so he went along with Holly and her insanity. At least until the night of the banquet when he told her she needed to figure out a plan because he was done playing the game."

That news made Mag's heart go pitter-pat. "What did Holly say?"

"She said a public breakup would be good publicity, but we needed to wait for just the right time. He thought she was stringing him along, I disagreed, and we fought. Holly's good at her job and I know she had our best interests in mind, so on a professional level, I understood the necessity. But on a personal one, I hated every minute of it."

Trying to ignore Clara fluttering about the room, Mag let Grace continue.

"It's not as though co-host on an adventure network was ever my dream job. Except for the travel, and the fact that I got to share it with Kevin. Now that he's gone, I won't be able to bear it. I've already given my resignation, and I can tell you it wasn't well-received. It's going to cost me a pretty penny to get out of my contract, but I don't care anymore."

"Do you have any idea who killed him?"

"God's truth, I don't. Kevin was the kind of man who would not only hand-deliver soup to a sick co-worker but would come to work early and stay late to fill in and make sure the show ran smoothly. He loved his job, and he was good at it. The worst thing he ever did was let someone else win a race."

"Who knows about your resignation?" For the life of her, Mag couldn't see a scenario where Grace resigning would cause someone to attack Matt, but she'd grasp at straws if it helped unravel the case.

"Holly, Skip, and the network brass, for now. I was going to make an announcement when this shoot ended. I told Matty last night, but now that he's been hurt, I don't know if I can go on."

How the woman could eat this many bags of chips and still look like a stick figure, Clara did not know, but as she scrunched yet another empty sack into the trash, she asked, "What was his state of mind after you talked?"

"Listen, we're friendly, but he was as sick of the charade as I was. He was thrilled to be out of it, and it didn't hurt that he'd be taking over the show on his own. Finally being able to take his marriage out of the closet was the cherry on the sundae. When he left me, he had the first real smile on his face I've seen since Kevin died."

That tracked with everything they'd learned so far.

"Did anyone else know about Matt and Jane? And when did they tell you?"

"I only found out last night, but Matt said Holly knew. No surprise there, but she kept a tight lid on it. I'm not sure if anyone else did. Maybe Skip, but you'd have to ask him."

"Is that the only thing you talked about last night?" Mag interjected.

Grace raised a perfectly tweezed eyebrow, "Maybe you ladies actually *will* solve this crime. You seem to know far more than you ought to. No, there's more to the story." She sighed, "I'm ashamed to say I thought Matt might have been responsible for Kevin's death."

"Why would you think that?" Clara asked.

Grace shrugged. "We really were a couple at one time and I wondered if Matt wanted to start things up again. In my defense, I didn't know about Jane, and Matt suspected me, too."

"A lot of that going around. Hiding out hasn't made you the picture of innocence." If people saw the state of this room, Clara thought, her reputation for being all put together would be shot, too.

"Matt saw me fighting with Kevin the night he died. The last thing I said to him was out of anger, and that's going to haunt me for the rest of my life. Maybe if I hadn't kicked him out of my room that night, he'd still be alive."

As if out of reflex, Grace moved toward the mini-bar and selected a bag of peanuts. Shaking fingers tore the bag open and she shoveled a scant handful into her mouth.

"You're not guilty of anything." Sympathy welled up in Clara, and she took it upon herself to gently pull the peanuts away from Grace. "And eating junk isn't going to help you face the loss."

Always ready with the hugs, Clara offered one now. Probably the first genuine bit of comfort Grace had received since her loss. Her arms went around Clara like a vise.

"Thank you. For everything."

"What do you think, Clarie?" Mag asked after she and Clara had changed back into their regular clothes.

"I'm honestly surprised Grace had no clue about Matt and Jane. That woman is a hell of a lot smarter than

anyone gives her credit for, and a gifted actress to boot.”
Clara replied.

Mag agreed, “She sure is. Which is what worries
me. If she and Matt both suspected one another of killing
Kevin, what evidence did Matthew have? Did he know
something we don’t? And she didn’t come clean about
why she thought he’d been the one.”

“It made sense to me,” Clara said. “Grace has been
virtually locked in her room with nothing but her
thoughts for days now. It’s easy for the imagination to
take wild flights of fancy when a person is stuck inside
their own head.”

“I suppose. If I hadn’t seen her turn it on for the
cameras the other day, I’d find it easier to buy the whole
*distraught and not thinking right* thing.”

“Let’s say you’re right, and she’s lying,” Clara said,
playing devil’s advocate. “Do you really see Grace as a
cold-hearted snake who killed her own lover, and then
attacked his best friend when he figured out she did it?”

“Well, when you put it like that, I guess not.”

“Then, she’s got two random women who know far
too much sneaking into her hotel room under somewhat
suspicious circumstances. I’m thinking she’d have had a
much different reaction than to spill her guts to us.”

“I know, and Janie’s story corroborates her version
of the conversation with Matt.” Mag gave in and threw
up her hands. “And now we’re back to square one.
Unless we’ve poked enough bears to have one of them
show up on our back porch with a machete.”

"Then, it's a good thing we're powerful witches, fully capable of protecting ourselves then." Clara seriously doubted it would come to that, but stranger things had happened. In fact, stranger things happened to her and her sister on a regular basis, so perhaps Mag was right to be paranoid and overly cautious.

"Can we go to the hospital and check on Matt?" Worry creased Mag's brow, she really had taken a shine to the man. "Kill two birds with one stone, and make sure Nye isn't investigating this as a suicide attempt."

"I think her investigative skills are improving. One of these days she might even solve a case without us to help."

"You think so? We'll see how you feel when the next dead body turns up."

Clara smacked her sister on the arm, "What do you mean, the next body? Maggie, I swear to the Goddess, you better find a piece of wood to knock on before everybody's little friend Kismet shows up. All I want to do is make lotions and soaps, and perhaps have time to do some, I don't know, *magic* every once in a while."

"Well, that's funny, because when you returned from the dead you said you were tired of standing in one place and wanted to see the world. We're barely outside the city limits of Port Harbor, and now you want to what? Dance skyclad around the ritual fire, then put your granny panties back on and go to crochet club? Come on, Clarie. You can enchant your stupid hook to self-crochet you a dozen afghans with a snap of your fingers. What gives?" Mag demanded and Clara knew she was taking the conversation down this road in order to keep her mind off hearing more bad news.

Clara glared at Mag, "What gives is that I was the Keeper for a hundred years, and I prefer routine to chaos. Are you happy? You're the adventurous one, the bird who jumps out of the nest too early but somehow still manages to fly. I play it safe. I wait until I'm ready before I make big changes. It's not a shortcoming, though I know you'll disagree."

"Oh, Clarie," Mag heaved an enormous sigh, "sometimes I think you don't really understand me at all."

# Chapter Sixteen

After running into the nursing equivalent of a linebacker at the hospital, the Balefire sisters returned home with no news about Matt's condition. To their surprise, Lynn Nye's car sat in the narrow driveway.

Mag huffed out a breath. "Nurse Ratched turned us in."

Clara paused before turning into the drive. "Well, what did you expect, Maggie? You called her that right to her face. Deputy Nye hasn't seen us yet, so you zip on ahead and get things ready."

Since this visit was probably her fault, Mag chose not to argue, but she was grumbling under her breath when she disappeared.

Slowing, Clara took her sweet time parking and gathering up her purse while Lynn waited patiently.

"Come on in, Deputy." Clara took a surreptitious look around, directing her gaze in the direction of Mrs. Green's dooryard, hoping the nosy old neighbor wasn't watching her usher the police inside yet again. "Would you like something to drink?" Nobody could call Clara Balefire inhospitable, that was for sure.

"Call me Lynn, I'm off the clock. And I'd love some of that iced tea of yours if you have any."

"Of course," Clara ushered the young officer inside, down a long hallway and into the parlor, displaying Mag's rusty entertaining skills.

With very little experience in setting a table for guests, Mag made a bullseye for her comfort zone and landed dead in the middle of the Victorian era.

She'd conjured a pitcher of tea that rested on a tray alongside a plate of finger sandwiches. Thin slivers of cucumber peeked out from between slices of fluffy white bread slathered with whipped cream cheese and a few sprigs of watercress. Mag's rocking chair creaked gently back and forth, and the whole picture looked like an old-fashioned painting.

"I'm sorry they wouldn't let you in to see Matt, but since you're not family and there was foul play involved, well, I hope you understand." The deputy explained.

Clara did, but her sister answered with a "harumph" and an annoyed expression.

Lynn took a sip of iced tea, a bite of the proffered sandwich, and then wiped the crumbs off her lap in a gesture that said it was time to get down to business. "So, let me start by saying that while I'm grateful for any information you can give me, I'm still a little concerned about Mayor McCreery asking you to insert yourselves into the investigation. Don't get me wrong," she said, holding up a hand. "It's not personal. I wish I had half your life experience, but that comes with time. I merely don't want to see either of you come to harm at the hands of a deranged murderer. I suppose there's nothing to be done about it now, this far in, but this second attack is concerning on more than one level. Please be careful."

Mag's eyes narrowed at the phrase 'half your life experience', considering Lynn Nye had no clue how many years that would amount to in actuality, but she kept her tone even as she replied, "We can take care of ourselves just fine, so don't you worry about that. Now, let's get to the brass tacks of it. We're at a dead end."

"Not a dead end, exactly," Clara interrupted, "More like a fork in the road, after the fork took a ride in the garbage disposal. The tines are all crooked and gnarled and curled around one another. From what we can tell, Matt had just gotten the first piece of good news he'd heard in a while. It makes no sense that he would have tried to kill himself."

"You're telling me." Lynn sighed. "You're right, you know. As usual. I'm not sure how the two of you are always right, but you've proved yourselves yet again. This wasn't a suicide." She paused to let her words sink in.

It took about a nanosecond before Mag fired back with her usual tact. "Well, duh. What finally tipped you off?"

Lynn chose to ignore the sarcasm. "For one thing, the trajectory of the bullet. Usually, if someone's intent really is to off themselves, they put the gun to their temple where it has the greatest chance of doing enough damage to end life immediately. In Matt's case, the bullet fired nearer to the back of his head, causing a hematoma but not fracturing the skull." Nye held her forefinger to her own head in explanation.

"See how awkward that would be? It's highly unlikely Matt did this to himself. His doctor said if they can get the swelling to go down, a full recovery might be possible." Deputy Nye held up a hand, "Don't get too excited, we're talking about a serious injury, and the odds of that happening are still overwhelmingly small."

Mag let the pessimistic comment slide right on by. "You said 'for one thing', so what else?"

"He had a drapery tie from the Oarhouse in his jacket pocket. I put a rush on forensics and the trace evidence confirmed my suspicions that it was, in fact, the one used to murder Kevin. If it weren't for the physical evidence, him hanging onto it out of guilt might make sense." Nye explained.

"But under these circumstances, it looks like a setup perpetrated by Kevin's actual killer." Clara finished for her. "Except he was seen in the room where the pistol was kept. Why? And what happened between last night and this morning? Why was he even down by the water in the first place."

"He was obviously lured there by our murderer." Mag didn't use the word 'duh' this time, but the sentiment was implied nonetheless. "And since we're pretty certain it was neither Jane nor Grace, that only leaves Holly or Skip, our two guiltiest-looking suspects from the beginning."

Nye's expression turned stony, "And this is where the two of you bow out. Leave the rest to me. The last thing we need is for you two to pull another Batman and Robin. You might have an in with Mayor McCreery, but you're not cops and you're not private investigators. Therefore, technically, you're vigilantes, and that's the kind of press this story doesn't need."

Clara and Mag put on their most convincing masks of resignation and dutifully agreed to all of Deputy Nye's demands before walking her to the front door and bidding her goodbye.

"So, which one of us is Batman, and which of us is Robin?" Mag asked with a straight face once Lynn was out of earshot.

Clara raised an eyebrow, "I ain't nobody's sidekick, I can promise you that, Maggie."

*We'll see about that, Clarie*, Mag thought to herself, vowing to settle up with her sister once they'd finished helping the Harmony police solve yet another crime.


With the waterlogged cast and crew holed up back at the Oarhouse, Mag and Clara knew just where to find Skip. Her hand poised to knock, Mag paused when she heard two voices coming from behind the door of his room, shrugged, and pulled out the earphones she'd decided to nick from her sister.

"I don't think you understand the amount of pressure I'm under!" Skip whined, having reverted back to the limp-livered little boy the Balefires had already suspected him to be.

"Who do you think he's talking to?" Clara whispered.

Her question was answered a moment later when Holly scoffed, "Oh, really? *I* don't know what kind of pressure *you're* under? Do you have any idea who you're talking to? You've been on the job for a week, and you're already melting under the heat of corporate's gaze. How do you think I feel? I've had to navigate so many land mines the last few months, it's a wonder I've still got all my limbs."

"Maybe it's just not worth it after all. They're expecting some kind of miracle, and I'm fresh out." Skip said. "And it's not like it's going to change anything anyway. The show is doomed without Matt, and it'll take an act of God to ensure he pulls through."

Before Holly could respond, Skip's phone rang again. "Hello?" He was quiet for a second, then said, "No, it's still raining, and the water level is still too high." He paused, "I don't have an answer about that yet, either. It's only been an hour. Do you think there are suitable co-host candidates just littering the streets of this backwoods town? Send someone down here. That's the solution." Skip listened for a moment and then let out a resigned sigh. "Fine, I'll see what I can do. But don't say I didn't warn you."

"That old saying about there being no business like show business was spot-on, huh?" Mag nudged her sister. "Things were so much simpler back in our day. No wonder old Haggie has gone wackadoo."

Clara grinned, "She's probably quite sane if you think about it from the perspective that she's got a thousand years' worth of detritus rolling around in her brain."

Mag hushed her as the voices resumed.

"Why don't you just ask one of the judges, Skipper?" Holly asked.

Skip's voice dropped an octave. "Don't call me Skipper, Holly. I mean it. And which one? We're down to just Grant Garnett and Jason Trumbell, and Grant's a sponsor, so unless I can get a waiver it's a conflict of interest."

"What about Jason?" she asked, a concerned edge to her tone.

Skip considered the question. "I highly doubt Jason will agree. It took a lot of cajoling to get him to agree to come in the first place, and I think the only reason he did was because *nobody* ever told Kevin Cardiff no."

"I agree," Holly said. "Jason's probably a long shot. I overheard him telling Grant that winning that race was the worst thing that ever happened to him. Only rich bastards complain about trophies and endorsement deals. No offense."

"None taken. I wouldn't even be here if my father weren't holding my trust fund ransom. Believe me. If I don't succeed, I might as well kiss it goodbye. Damn whoever killed Kevin. And damn Matty, too. Coward's way out, if you ask me." Skip's voice held disdain and a little something that resembled sadness.

Clara raised an eyebrow, "Maybe old Skip's part human after all."

Holly sighed heavily. "We're going to have to divide and conquer. We can't even shoot if both Grace and Matt are out of the picture. Obviously, there's nothing *you* are going to be able to say to Grace that will convince her to stay on for even one more episode. But I might have a shot. Still, there's nothing I can do about the rain unless you know some kind of anti-rain dance."

"So we divide and conquer. I'll keep searching for a replacement for Matt, and I'll submit for the waiver in case Grant says yes." Skip sounded about as thrilled as if someone had asked him to shovel horse manure all day. "It's all a moot point if the weather doesn't clear up, though." He barked out a laugh. "Maybe one of these backwater hippies knows how to make it stop raining."

Mag snorted. "And maybe Skip's not human at all. What a jerk. I'd like to—" Mag's diatribe cut off before it could even begin, leaving Clara wondering what kind of toad she'd make out of Skip if she had the chance. The last few pieces of Mag's puzzle were still waiting to fall into place, but she could finally see what the big picture was going to be.

"Clarie, it's been staring us in the face all along."

Clara quickly thought through the myriad information they'd learned recently, while a niggling feeling that she'd missed something obvious settled into her gut. "What, Maggie?"

"Skip is just a jerk. Holly is just a PR rep with a horrible job. They may have looked suspicious, but only because we kept thinking something happened to upset Matt between last night and this morning. But he didn't try to kill himself. Because he wasn't upset about anything!" The words tumbled from Mag's mouth.

Finally understanding, Clara bowed her head shamefully. "Jason's the one who said that. And Jason is also the only person to give any real evidence in Kevin's murder. The mysterious Trek employee who followed Kevin to the pool."

"Right, but there was no Trek employee. He's been trying to sidetrack the cops so they don't figure out it was him all along. But why?" Mag still didn't have the answer to the question of motive.

"Whatever the reason," Mag continued, "it's tied to why he had to be dragged back into this scene kicking and screaming. I have a sneaking suspicion it's related to all these cryptic comments about Kevin and Matt throwing the Backwater Paddle ten years ago."

She stomped back down the hallway and descended the stairs into the front lobby, her brain spinning with the implication.

Clara followed. "What I don't understand is the same thing that's bothering Holly. Why would Jason be so angry about a race he actually *won*? I'd like to think it took more than sheer vanity to push him toward murder. Who knew the canoe racing circuit was filled with so much drama and intrigue?"

Mag shook her head, "Definitely not me, but I don't know why you're shocked, Soap Opera Queen. You've filled the DVR again, by the way."

Clara ignored her sister's complaint, "What now?"

"Well, we can't just waltz up to Jason and demand an explanation. We'll need a plan, and right now we don't have time for that." Mag said, matter-of-factly.

Clara arched a brow. "You have some other important plans I don't know about? Is the Queen of Faerie coming to dinner?"

"We have to take care of the rain," Mag said, rolling her eyes as if Clara had missed the obvious. "Skip was right—this backwater hippie has a few tricks up her sleeve. If Matt wakes up, I want him to still have a job, and every second we let it pour down in sheets makes that less and less likely. What do you say, Clarie?"

"Far be it from me to stop you from doing something nice for someone. Particularly someone you just met and barely know. I think you're growing, Maggie."

"Eat dirt, Clara."

# Chapter Seventeen

"Do you think they'll call off the race?" It was the question of the day, muttered by everybody in town, it seemed. Every customer through the door wanted to gossip about the murders and lament about the weather.

With the rain still coming down in sheets it seemed the weather war Hagatha had begun with the pixies was still in effect. Unfortunately, with Hagatha missing, neither side was available to make it end. That left it up to Clara and Mag to clean up the mess, which was becoming par for the course.

Weather spells were tricky enough to be saved for those times when absolutely necessary, and only when the cost of working them was outweighed by the gain. In other words, almost never.

Mother Nature, when prodded, tended to retaliate in the worst possible way. Mag maintained the queen of the woodland sprites had a perpetual case of PMS and took out her moods on the world whenever she lost a bet with Father Time.

Father Time let it be known that Mother Nature was an easy mark after she took a sucker bet on whether a grasshopper would jump left or right, and it snowed in Maine in June that year.

"How are we going to fix this?" Mag, carrying a striped umbrella, followed Clara as she harvested rosemary and mint for a batch of rejuvenating foot scrub. "My herb beds are hanging on by a thread at this point."

A fat slug left a juicy trail of slime over Mag's shoe, and when she shook it off, it splatted against the patio stones. "I'm not sure. I've been turning it over in my head since yesterday, and I've got nothing. Except motivation to help poor Matt. What really gets my goat is that Hagatha's not even here anymore, and we're still putting out fires."

"Ooh, would that work, do you think?"

Mag searched her memory for some idea of what she'd just said that would spark the question. Finding nothing, she gave in and asked, "Would what work?"

"Putting out the Balefire for just long enough to break the spell."

Mag spun on her. "Clara Balefire, have you lost complete control of your faculties? We can't put out the Balefire. That would be madness."

"Well, let it dwindle down to embers, then," Clara said. "Not all the way out, but enough to weaken the spell. Otherwise, we're going to have to ask for help, and that means telling the coven about Hagatha and the pixies. I mean, I know they know she had them, but they don't know we didn't make her get rid of them sooner."

"This was not our fault." Mag shook her head. "Honestly, Clarie, I think you developed some sort of martyr complex during your unfortunate incarceration. Hagatha was … is her own worst enemy, and we are not responsible for every hair-brained scheme she dreams up.”

Mag's right hand tapped against her thigh impatiently. "But, I suppose you're right about one thing. We're going to have to swallow our pride and tell the coven something to explain her absence. It might as well be the truth, and they can work with us to stop the rain whether they want to or not. For Matty's sake.”

Now that she'd decided on this course of action, Mag would waste no time setting things in motion. "And if you think I'm going to eat crow over this, you'll be bellying up to that meal by yourself.”

With as much dignity as she could muster walking through the soggy gardens, Mag swept toward the house, leaving Clara lost in thought.

Was Mag right? Had she become timid while frozen in place with nothing to do but think about every mistake she'd ever made?

Parts of her still felt encased in stone. That much she could admit if only to herself. Little pebbles lodged deep in the heart of her, and like the pea under the mattress of the princess caused niggling discomfort.

Too much introspection, she decided, wasn't good for the soul. It made one pick away at the frayed spots until all the threads unraveled. No one came back from that type of thing and just took up their lives as though nothing had happened.

"Looks like I brought more baggage to Harmony than just my clothes," Clara muttered. "And I'll probably have to unpack a few things."

Resolute, she followed in the direction her sister had taken.

"Maggie, you're right," she said when she caught up. "We don't owe Penelope or the coven anything other than our help."

"Good, because I already sent out a summons through the Balefire, and we're all meeting in Dawkin's woods in half an hour."

"Weather spells aren't that difficult to work," Evanora Dupree, one of Penelope's henchwomen spat the misleading statement in a snarky tone, her lip curled. "I don't see why you needed to call us all here like this. You're the almighty Balefires; you should be able to stop a little rain by yourselves." The implication—and it was one Mag had heard more than once since moving to town—was that this was just another dirty job the rest of the coven shouldn't be bothered with.

She fixed the witch with her best withering stare and opened her mouth to make a scathing retort. Before the first word formed on her lips, Clara's voice chilled the air.

"Goddess knows I've tried to fit in and to be tolerant, but my patience has worn thinner than onion skin." Little sparks of power sizzled from Clara's clenched fists where they hung at her side and dribbled like water to the ground.

The static energy lifted strands of silky chestnut to wave around her head. The sight made Mag grin and want to clap her hands. If she wasn't mistaken, Clara was back and there was about to be hell to pay.

"I'm not sure what Penelope told you, or what you've heard about me or my sister, but if you think we came here to work off some karmic debt, or because we were no longer welcome in Port Harbor, then you've got it all wrong."

The number of eyes that shifted away from Clara's level gaze confirmed her suspicions.

"I see. Well, let's clear up a few misconceptions here and now. Not only have we mended fences with Calypso Snodgrass, who is a fine high priestess, by the way, but we also share a family bond."

As shock registered on some faces, Clara's mouth slanted into a mirthless grin. She turned her eyes up and to the right to grab the next vicious rumor from the list.

"And I know people are saying my granddaughter kicked me out of the house so she could be Keeper of the Flame." More eyes turned away.

"I never believed that for a minute." Gertrude pulled the candy cane out of her mouth long enough to speak vehemently. "Not for a single minute. Anyone could see she's a sweet girl with a fine disposition who would never turn her back on family that way."

Certain points of emphasis called Clara's disposition into question.

Light dawned in her eyes. "But you think I would." She huffed out a disgusted breath. "And if I'd turn my back on family, then I'd turn my back on my coven just as willingly. I see."

Resisting the temptation to jump to Clara's defense, Mag waited for her sister to take fire. The Clara she remembered had been full of sass, and while tender-hearted, never a pushover.

It had taken a flaming arrow to pierce Clara's cold, stone heart and set it beating once again, but it hadn't been enough to dispel the shadows behind her eyes. Mag knew it would take a rekindling of her sister's inner light, and hoped a bout of self-righteous anger would be the catalyst.

"We've already hashed out the question of my *supposed* guilt in the *supposed* death of my daughter, who is very much alive, so I assume we can all let that one go." Biting off the words, Clara paced before the assembled group. "Am I right?"

Heat, and power, and magic pumped off her body to tingle through the clearing and set the coven's collective teeth on edge. If any of them had forgotten the wealth of power commanded by a Balefire witch, even if she wasn't the reigning Keeper of the Sacred Flame, they remembered it now.

Penelope's face looked like it had been chiseled out of marble, and Mag wondered which rode the other witch harder, embarrassment or fear. Either one was fine with her because she'd had about enough sanctimony for one lifetime.

For one, long and satisfying moment, Mag let her own magic build to something close to its true potential, sent it to mingle with Clara's. It was about time the coven got a taste of the Balefire legacy. Right at the point of where tolerance found its edge, she clapped her hands, and let the magic dissipate.

"This will be the last time we have this discussion." Mag's voice echoed like thunder, and she let the moment play out long before speaking again—in her normal tone.

"Hagatha Crow is no longer with us."

If Mag had dropped a bomb in the middle of the sacred circle, it would have caused less of a stir, and it tickled her no end to see the consternation she'd caused with that one statement.

"Thanks, Maggie." Clara's quiet comment referred to the show of support, not the breaking of the Hagatha news, but she noted which witches showed genuine sorrow and the number was higher than she'd have guessed.

"No, she's not dead. Or I don't think she's dead, anyway." Mag held up a hand to stop the barrage of questions and then launched into the story of Hagatha and the pixies.

"And now, we're all going to work together, *as a coven*, to break the spell." The emphasis drove home the point and presenting her fiercest face to the group quelled any rebellion.

After calling the corners and appealing to the relevant goddesses, the final words of the spell echoed into silence and the coven waited as the world around them seemed to take a breath. And then erupted into chaos.

Wind flared, rain slanted nearly sideways, and lightning forked into the center of the circle, leaving the air burning with the sulfurous scent of ozone. Half the witches ran for cover, the rest just stood there looking shocked.

"Well, that didn't work." Ever the queen of the understatement, Mag blew a drop of rain off the end of her nose and dodged another bolt of lightning. "I can't believe I'm saying this, but I wish Hagatha were here. Or just a bit of her essence, and we need something from the pixies, too. Maybe we missed a feather when we cleaned up the compound."

"For Hecate's sake. I'm a complete idiot sometimes." Clara fished around in her bag and pulled out one of the glass beads from the portal spell. It still had a smear of Hagatha's blood on it. "Will this work?" She handed it over and drove her hand into the bag to fish around for a second item, finally producing a small vial of pixie honey.

"You call me a packrat," Mag said, "but you might have just saved the day."

Bolstered by what magic remained in the sample of Hagatha's blood, the spell ended, and as abruptly as twisting a faucet handle, so did the rain.

Sudden quiet fell over the clearing as the sun broke through the clouds to send gentle fingers toward the earth, and then an excited chatter broke out among the witches.

"Well done, you lot." Dead silence descended again when the unmistakable creak of Hagatha Crow's voice came out of a seemingly empty space. As if pushed through a doorway, she stumbled into visibility and looked around with a satisfied grin. "About time you put yourselves to use."

# Chapter Eighteen

Hagatha's refusal to discuss her sojourn in the land of the Fae wore through Mag's nerves in less than five minutes. Mag's refusal to let it go wore through Clara's in less time than that.

To avoid casting a muzzle spell that was sure to go horribly wrong, she stepped up her pace and got far enough ahead that the bickering faded into the background. Sun angled through dissipating clouds, warming the back of Clara's neck, and bringing out a swarm of mosquitoes to buzz and hum.

Wherever the sun's heat touched the damp earth, mists gathered and swirled—not unlike the thoughts and impressions of the past week that chased through Clara's head.

If Kevin's death benefited Jason, Clara couldn't see how, and with nothing to gain, the motive for killing him was as clear as a bug-stained windshield. She swatted the thousandth mosquito from her arm; it seemed she had insects on the brain.

Money, love, or revenge. As Mag always said, those were the three main motives for murder. Taking them in order and considering Jason as the murderer, money or love were easy enough to rule out.

Revenge fit the ferocious and deeply personal nature of the crime and was harder to pin down than a leaf in an autumn wind. Probably some small slight had lodged like a splinter and festered. But for ten years?

Cranky voices and their owners followed Clara all the way back to the van, where she took the driver's seat—much to Mag's annoyance—and drove back to the inn instead of the store.

"I just want to check the water levels. Do you mind, Hagatha?" As lies went, this one was white enough to blend into a winter day, and Mag wasn't fooled one tiny bit. "You've had some sort of epiphany about Jason."

"No, not as such," Clara said, keeping her eyes on the road. "I'm just thinking about possible motives because it doesn't make sense."

"Revenge." Mag clued right in. "What do we know about Kevin's past that might make him a target?"

"Not just Kevin. With the attack on Matt, the only thing I can think of is them throwing that canoe race ten years ago. Doesn't make sense, though, because didn't Jason benefit?"

"One man's triumph is another man's heartbreak." Hagatha's voice creaked out from the back of the van like a rusty old gate hinge.

Kevin was already dead, and Matt was safely ensconced in the ICU, so why did Clara feel such an urgency to find Grant or Jason and ferret out the truth? No one else should be in danger, but the screaming need settled in the pit of her stomach and made her drive faster.

Mag approved.

"About time you learned where the gas pedal is," she crowed.

"The van runs on magic, so technically, there is no gas.."

Magic was the only thing that kept the tires firmly on the road when Clara screeched through the curved entrance to the inn. A flick of intention opened up a parking space that hadn't been there a moment before, and the bus was still settling into it when Clara's feet landed on the pavement.

"Don't say a word," Clara warned her sister. "Not one single word." Working a spell in public would be the least of her problems if this sinking feeling of dread was anything to go by.

Powerful magic oozed out of Clara's pores and sent out a static charge. Something of her urgency must have carried over because Mag began to feel it, too.

They found Grant sitting by the pool. "Any news?" He asked.

"He's still listed in critical condition," Worry hushed Mag's voice.

"I've been over it and over it in my head. I saw Matt that morning and I didn't suspect a thing. Feel bad, you know? I should have noticed something. Might have been able to stop it, stop him. Something."

"You're a good person, Grant." Clara believed that and because she did, she felt compelled to say, "Tell me about your history with Matt, and the other race." The key to the present mystery lay somewhere in the past.

"Winning that race changed my life. We got the endorsement deal, which sounds loftier than it was. Rockapotamus was a small company then, just starting out, so it amounted to little more than a few bucks here and there and a free trip to wherever they were filming the next advertisements. We got to meet a few babes in bikinis, so there were some perks."

Grant pulled out his wallet and showed off a photo of his wife and their current brood. "I met the love of my life on one of those shoots, and then ended up with a great job working for the company. Whatever prompted Kevin and Matt to bow out, I will be forever grateful to them."

With that, Grant took himself out of the running as a suspect, which left only one other option.

"And Jason? Did he feel the same?"

Stunned silence followed on the heels of Grant's knee-jerk affirmative. "No," He amended, "Jason had a run of bad luck after the race. He lost a good job because of all the travel, and the deal didn't pay enough to make up for the work. His fiancée was a gem, though. She agreed to put off the wedding date and supported him all the way. Hell of a woman."

Fingers rasping over a day's worth of scruff, Grant scrubbed at his cheek in an absent-minded way. "We missed a flight from the west coast on a Friday afternoon because the shoot ran long, and we couldn't get another one until later that evening."

He paused long enough for Clara to prod. "And then what?"

"We landed and she wasn't there to meet the plane, but Jason wasn't worried. Not then, anyway. He figured she'd taken a later shift, so I gave him a lift home. I saw the blue lights flashing, but the cop cars were down the street, so I didn't think anything of it, dropped him off and left."

Clearing a voice gone rough with emotion, Grant continued. "If I'd known, I wouldn't have left him there alone. Hope had clocked out of work, and her car wouldn't start, so she left it there, and decided to walk home and take his. Her job was only a mile from the house, but she'd been planning to drive to the airport right from work, so she took the car that day."

Mag shifted in her seat and earned herself a quelling look from Clara. If the story was this painful for Grant, how much more must Jason have suffered? None of that was a good enough excuse for murder or attempted murder, but it didn't take a genius or an Olympic-level mental leap to solve the crime now.

"Hit and run. That's what the police said. She never saw it coming. A Good Samaritan saw the whole thing and called an ambulance. The docs did everything they could, but she didn't make it."

Standing abruptly, Grant put the pieces together for himself.

"You think Jason killed Kevin." Blunt fingers speared through hair already mussed. Muscles coiled like springs, Grant paced the short distance between the table and the fence around the pool.

"God help me, I think you're right." He dropped back into his chair.

"Do you know where Jason is?" The thrill of the chase settled on her, and Mag never even considered calling Lynn Nye.

"He went to check the water level. Should have been back by now."

"Thanks. We'll go see if we can find him." Standing to leave, Clara was aware how it might look to an outsider. One woman bordering on middle age, accompanied by two more who were long past the chase-down-a-bad-guy phase of life.

"You're not going alone. He's killed one man and nearly killed another." Any man who had a lick of common sense would have left off the last sentence, but Grant kept right on talking. "What are you three going to do if he tries something?"

"I vote for turning him into a slug and stepping on him, but these two never let me have any fun." Grant spared Hagatha a look then turned to Clara as if the old woman had proved his point for him.

With the cocksure righteousness only a man with a case of the smugs could carry off, Grant unlatched the gate at the side of the pool and made for the trail leading down to the river.

They met Jason coming the other way about halfway between the dock and the fork in the path leading toward town.

"Hey Jase, we were just looking for you." If Grant had a poker face, he forgot to pack it for the trip because Jason took one look at him and bolted.

"Sorry, Maggie." When Grant launched after him, Clara followed suit and, long legs flashing, quickly left her companions behind. The pair reached the dock just in time to see Jason's paddle flashing through the water as he turned the bow of the canoe downstream.

"He's getting away." Magic could have stopped Jason, but before Clara could work out the proper spell to throw, Grant was grabbing another canoe from the rack, so she opted for alerting the police instead.

"Come on." He braced the canoe while she shoved her phone back into her pocket, climbed in and settled herself, then he handed her a paddle and pushed off into the stream. "I think I can talk sense into him if we can catch up. Jason's not a bad guy."

"He's murdered one person in cold blood and tried to kill a second." Pointing out the obvious, Clara applied paddle to water and glanced back at the dock. A grim-faced Mag had arrived with Hagatha in tow, and the two of them were in the process of wrestling a third canoe into the water.

"No, Maggie! The water's too choppy. Stay there where it's safe."

Stopping long enough to flash her sister a rude hand gesture, Mag continued the awkward task of getting herself and Hagatha settled and ready to join the chase.

Meanwhile, Grant handled the canoe like a master, and with Clara's help, closed some of the distance between them and Jason, who battled the current alone.

"Jase, come on," he called. "I know there's got to be an explanation for what happened. You're not a killer, buddy, am I right? Let me help you. We'll talk to the police and get this whole thing sorted out."

"You don't know anything about it or about me," Jason shouted back and paddled harder as the canoe plunged through the water. "Now get back. I have a flare gun and I don't want to have to shoot you."

# Chapter Nineteen

"Paddle faster, you old coot," Mag told Hagatha. "I want to catch up to them." Concern for her sister loaned her the strength to pour on the speed, but Hagatha's response was to toss her paddle overboard.

"What are you doing?" Mag shouted. She might be stronger than she looked, but now Hagatha was so much dead weight and Mag's arms felt the strain. "I ought to throw *you* over the side."

"Or you could use magic like a proper witch. Get me close enough and I'll hex the son of a biscuit into the middle of next week."

Lagging farther behind wasn't an option Mag wanted to consider. She had a bad feeling about this. Not a premonition, and there hadn't been time for any sort of divination, but she trusted her gut enough to take Hagatha's advice.

"Velocitas," she whispered, and the next stroke of the paddle sent the canoe leaping forward.

"That's more like it." A fine spray of water arced up from the prow of the canoe to cast diamond-glinting droplets over Hagatha, who didn't seem at all bothered. "Faster. Make it fly."

"You're not going to shoot me." Clara hoped Grant was as certain as he sounded since she was in the line of fire. "And I'm not going away, so if you *are* going to fire that flare gun, do it and get it over with."

"Shut up—you're making it worse," she hissed at him, then kept on paddling, composing a shielding spell on the fly. Swollen with rain, Big Spurwink tossed the canoe around as if it weighed no more than a cork. That made them a moving target, but Clara wasn't taking any chances.

Not that she had much confidence in her ability to craft a well-honed spell while on water—she was a Balefire witch, after all, with an affinity for fire magic, and it was no secret water and fire don't mix.

Grant ignored the order and paddled harder. "Why did you do it, Jase? Help me understand what would push you to commit murder."

"Winning that race cost me Hope and she was everything," Jason yelled over his shoulder, his back straining as he paddled. "They wouldn't let me see her because I wasn't family. We put off the wedding so I could chase fame, and I didn't get to say goodbye or hold her hand. Hope died alone because Kevin and Matt cheated. I balanced the scales."

"You have to turn yourself in. This isn't what Hope would have wanted."

"Don't talk about her." Spit flew with the force of Jason's scream. The mask fell off his madness, and he raged. "Why are you defending them? Or maybe you were in on it too."

"That's a stupid thing to say."

"You're just making it worse," Clara admonished Grant in a low voice.

At her best guess, they had another five minutes before hitting the wide stretch of river behind the park. The police ought to be there by now, but there was still a chance Jason would get past them and into the rapids beyond.

Swollen by days and days of rain, the treacherous stretch of fast-moving water would either spit him out with a heck of a lead on the cops or kill him. They had to stop him before either of those things happened.


Mag dipped the bespelled paddle in the water and closed the distance by a few more feet. The stealth provided by one of Clara's silencing charms kept Jason from noticing the two witches closing into flanking position.

"Just get me close enough, and I'll take care the little pipsqueak," Hagatha leaned forward avidly.

"Working on it." Even with the magical help, Mag's breath had begun to puff. "You could have hung on to your paddle and helped a little."

"I'm the brains, you're the muscle."

192

Mag resisted the temptation to whack Haggie with the paddle, but only just, and turned her annoyance into more forward motion. When Jason started screaming that Grant must have been in on the conspiracy to ruin his life, she felt the hunter inside her start to stir.

Up through skin and bone and sinew came the primal lust for prey. This was something Clara would never understand. She was too pure of heart to feel the lure, the dark pulse of blood heating to the point of thrill from the scent of the hunted.

"He fires that gun, you handle it, but Jason is mine." Some of that power and lust echoed through Mag's voice and Hagatha turned in surprise but never got the chance to comment.

It all happened fast. As the three canoes drifted out of the narrows and along the leading edge of town, Jason dropped his paddle, raised the flare gun and took aim.

Clara saw the barrel like a dark eye searching for her, and poured more Balefire into her shield. Keeping Grant safe came first. She'd wipe his memory later and not count the cost to her own.

Jason shrieked something barely intelligible and tightened his finger on the trigger.

Time slowed to a crawl. Not because that often feels like the case in those situations, but because Hagatha pulled out some of her best magics and made it so.

A throaty growl rolled across the river, Mag gave one mighty pull on the paddle and brought the canoe into range.

Jason squeezed harder. Hagatha muttered something that sounded like *abracadabra,* which was impossible because no witch worth her salt would ever stoop so low. The flare gun went off at roughly the same time Mag's spell hit Jason in the back.

Instead of a flare, what came out of the gun was one of those flags with the word *bang* printed on it. Jason crumpled like a folded fan, and Clara dropped the shield.

"Is he dead? Maggie, you didn't, did you?"

"He's out cold." He could have been taken down by the chill in her tone as easily as whatever magic she'd used on him. "You okay?" Her gaze traveled, for the first time, toward Grant who was just dragging himself back up onto the seat after having dived into the bottom of the canoe in self-defense.

"What happened?" He took away the need for messing with his memory, and Clara sighed with relief.

"Doesn't matter. It's over now, and everyone's safe."

Deputy Nye arrived just in time to hear Clara's statement, her face a mix of relief and irritation. "I'm not even going to ask why you didn't call me sooner. You're lucky nobody got hurt, or you'd be in some serious trouble."

"It's not our fault he fled. What were we supposed to do, let him get away?" Mag asked, her tone iron. She wasn't one for being admonished for a job well done.

The deputy ignored her and descended upon the unconscious culprit, slapping a pair of handcuffs on

Jason before accepting Grant and Clara's help to get him on his feet.

As the ambulance screamed into the parking lot of Spurwink Park, Jason's eyes popped open and Clara could see the look of horror in his eyes as he replayed the events that had just transpired. His gaze flicked to Grant, whose face held a scathing expression.

"You almost just made a widow out of my wife, Jason." Grant spat. "How is that any fairer than you losing Hope? It might have been Kevin and Matt's fault we lost that race, but it was someone else's fault we missed our flight that day. What's more, you don't know how any of it would have played out under different circumstances. That's how life works. Now you've merely spread your misery around." Grant looked at Jason, his eyes pleading for some explanation he could understand.

"I've spent the last ten years wishing I hadn't won that race," Jason said, his expression a mix of anguish and disgust. "That's where it all started for me. And then I agreed to judge this race, thinking it was a chance for me to finally move on, and I learn that it all could have been different. If only Matt and Grant had accepted those poly-core paddles and won like they were slated to. I snapped. That's all I have to say. Please, Officer, just take me to jail. I'm prepared to make a full confession."

# Chapter Twenty

For the first time in weeks, Mag and Clara's sunrise walk felt cool and breezy, the way a summer morning should before the heat becomes stifling and clothes melt against skin. It was the kind of morning that had Clara making a mental list of possible tasks that, once the sun reached its peak, would be rendered useless yet still satisfying to have contemplated.

Jason was brought to justice, and his confession assured he'd remain behind bars for the rest of his life. Even though Clara knew he deserved it, part of her felt sorry for the man. Grief and pain could turn even the gentlest of souls into monsters—of that she was positive. Clara had let emotion get the best of her, and she'd had to pay the price, but it was difficult for her to wish for anyone to have to go through what she had, even if Jason did deserve to pay his own.

Mag, on the other hand, had no such qualms. In her mind, Jason's book was closed, and she'd no intention of giving him or his fate another thought. Maybe his fiancée would have lived if he hadn't won that race, but she felt it just as likely that Jason's trajectory could have taken an infinite number of other routes. What mattered was that in this dimension, he'd taken another person's life and Mag could feel no sympathy for what she considered the highest level of evil.

"You look nice today." Clara's compliment held enough surprise to earn a glare from her sister. "You're not even wearing anything in a 70s print."

"You're really bringing down my good mood, Clarie." Mag retorted, stomping on ahead for a moment before her cane got caught in a bramble of pricker bushes.

Clara gently and wordlessly got her sister untangled, and continued on down the river trail toward their destination. It was finally time for the Backwater Paddle Race to commence, and both Balefires were eager to see how it would proceed given all of the recent upheavals at the Trek Network.

Spurwink Park was packed to the gills with spectators, camera crews, and participants, and the air buzzed with excitement. Under the shade of a canvas canopy, perched on the edge of a director's chair, sat Grace, looking radiant in a flowing navy-and-white striped summer dress. When she lifted her hand in a wave toward Mag and Clara, there was a peace in her eyes that let them both know she'd be all right in the end.

"Ouch," Mag complained when Clara grabbed her arm and dug her nails in for purchase. "What are you doing, you nut?"

"What did *you* do? That's the real question." Clara pointed up the hill toward the park, where Matt Chase ambled across the grass with Jane clinging to his arm.

A smile spread across Mag's face, "It looks like he's made quite the recovery."

"Miraculous recovery, you mean." Hagatha's voice startled Mag and Clara, not having heard her approach without the tennis ball-footed walker she usually dragged everywhere.

Clara's eyes narrowed to slits, "Miraculous, indeed. We'll talk about this later."

Matt caught sight of the trio and made a beeline in their direction, wrapping his arms around Mag in an unexpected hug. Clara could see the stain of crimson on her sister's cheek and had a sneaking suspicion she understood why Mag had made herself more presentable than usual.

"Janie told me all about your daring, white-water-rapid adventure. I can't thank you enough for what you did. We're practically strangers, and you risked your lives to bring Kevin's killer and my attacker to justice." Matt said, gratitude and admiration written all over his face.

Mag shrugged off the praise, "It was nothing, really."

"No, it wasn't." Jane shook her head with conviction. "And if you hadn't found my Matty when you did that morning, he might not have made it. None of the doctors can believe he pulled through as quickly as he did, but I'm not surprised." Her face glowed as she looked up into Matt's face, so full of love and admiration it almost felt like an intrusion to watch. "Love can work miracles."

Matt tore his eyes away from Jane's with effort. "They wanted to keep me for a few more days, but I told them I wasn't going to be some guinea pig, especially not when I've got a job to do. They're revamping the series with me as the host, and they agreed to pay Grace her severance as long as she co-hosted the Backwater Paddle. She got a part on a soap opera and said the change of pace was just what she was looking for. Seems things worked out for everyone, except poor Kev."

Settling into chairs in the VIP seating Matt arranged for them, Mag and Clara watched the canoes line up for the beginning of the race.

Matt flinched when the starter pistol went off, but that was nothing compared to Mag's reaction when Hagatha leaned in and asked, "Any idea what happened to my honey pixie hives?"

The End